DOUGHNUT DOLLIES

American Red Cross girls during World War II

A novel by Helen Airy

SANTA FE
NEW MEXICO

Dedicated to my Children:
James Airy, Bill Airy, Patricia Webster

All characters, incidents, and dialogue in this book are the products of the authors imagination and are not to be construed as real. Although this novel is based on historical events, depictions are fictional and any resemblance to actual events or persons, living or dead, are entirely coincidental.

Printed in the United States of America

10 9 8 7 6 5 4 3 2 1

Library of Congress Cataloging in Publication Data:

Airy, Helen, 1914-
Doughnut dollies: American Red Cross girls during World War II: a novel /by Helen Airy.
p. cm.
ISBN: 0-86534-104-4 (paper)
1. World War, 1939-1945--War work--Red Cross--Fiction. 2. World War, 1939-1945--Women--Fiction.
I. Title.
PS3551.159D68 1995
813'.54--dc20
95-7145
CIP

Published by SUNSTONE PRESS
Post Office Box 2321
Santa Fe, NM 87504-2321 / USA
(505) 988-4418 / *orders only* (800) 243-5644
FAX (505) 988-1025

Cover design by Patrick A. DeAloe

Chapter 1

SAYING GOOD-BYE

Lisa Medina, reporter on the staff of the San Francisco Examiner, was enjoying her day off. It was Saturday morning, December 7, 1941. She was sitting on the sofa in the living room of her apartment on Nob Hill overlooking beautiful San Francisco Bay. She was knitting a sweater, humming along with the music on her radio, and thinking about where she and Steve would be going that evening on their regular Saturday night date.

Lee Yoshimoto, Lisa's Japanese house-boy, was working in the kitchen. Lee was a quiet young man who worked efficiently and did not talk much. Lisa had hired him without question from a local employment agency, and he had been with her every Saturday morning for the past three months.

Suddenly, an excited voice came over the radio, breaking into the music program without apology: "Japanese war planes bombed the United States naval fleet at Pearl Harbor this morning at dawn."

As suddenly as it came in, the voice cut off, and the music continued. "Did I hear what I thought I heard?" she asked herself.

Shortly the voice was back on the radio, calmer this time, methodically relating details of the bombing at Pearl Harbor. Lisa called to Lee to come listen.

Lee stepped into the living room, and listened without comment, his arms folded in front of him. When the voice on the radio stopped, Lee said quietly: "I must leave."

Lisa was startled: "Why?" she asked.

"I am to report to the authorities."

Lisa was silent. She was trying to collect her thoughts that were scattering about frantically trying to comprehend what was happening to her world. "You won't be in trouble, will you?" she asked.

"No," Lee answered."At least I don't think so. But they'll probably intern me for the duration."

"You mean they'll put you in jail?"

"Probably in a camp of some kind until the war is over. But I have to report immediately or risk punishment."

"I'll pay you for the rest of the morning,"Lisa said, as she reached for her purse on the coffee table and took out a ten dollar bill which she handed to Lee.

"I'm sorry,"she said. "If there's anything I can do..."

"I'm sorry, too," Lee said as he turned towards the door.

Then he was gone, and Lisa never saw him again. After Lee left, a strange thought entered Lisa's mind. She really didn't know anything about Lee. Perhaps he might be one of the enemy. He seemed to know a lot about what was happening. Immediately she was ashamed of her suspicions, and vowed that she would never again allow herself to jump to conclusions without knowing the facts. Lisa was a reporter and that was the first thing you learned in the journalistic profession. Lee, she was sure, was even more of a victim than she. His education as a student at San Francisco State would be disrupted. Maybe he would be sent back to Japan and would be drafted into the Japanese army, or maybe as he said, he would be interned in the United States. Lisa was sorry that she hadn't asked Lee where she could reach him.

The phone rang. It was Steve calling. Steve was Lisa's concern now. Certainly he would be drafted. It was a thought that overwhelmed her. Within the last few minutes Lisa's life had been turned upside down.

"Have you heard the news?"Steve asked.

"Yes, I've heard."

"I'll be over."

Lisa hung up the phone in a daze. Steve was more than a friend. She and Steve had been a twosome for almost five years. They dated all through four years of college, and it was understood between them that shortly, as soon as Steve was established in a suitable job, they would marry. In the meantime Steve was living in an apartment he shared with his older sister, Jessica, who was a schoolteacher and Lisa's friend. There were no problems for Lisa and Steve. Everything was O.K. Until now....

Lisa opened the door at Steve's knock, and Steve took her in his arms and held her tight. Steve was a tall man, and ruggedly handsome. He was the kind of man Lisa had always admired. He was one who took command, and who always seemed to know the right path to take. Lisa depended upon him, and had never doubted that he would always be there when she needed him.

Steve led Lisa to the sofa, and when they were seated, he turned to her and held her face between his hands: "You know what this means?"

"Yes, it means you'll be leaving soon."

"That's right. I've been thinking about this for some time. I didn't expect it to happen so soon, and not this way, but I expected we would be at war soon. So there are some things I have to tell you."

Lisa was crying, and Steve was upset. He had seen Lisa cry only once before when she received word of her father's death. Steve took a handkerchief from his pocket and wiped her eyes. "Please don't cry, Lisa," he pleaded, "please. You know I love you. There isn't another girl for me, and none as beautiful."

Steve stroked Lisa's long dark hair, a special way he had of showing affection. "You've got everything a man could dream of," he continued. "You've got wonderful wavy brown hair, big brown eyes, a curvy figure, and a smile that always melts my heart and I know you've got guts. No matter what happens, I know you can take it."

Lisa stopped crying. "Thanks, Steve," she said. "I needed that. I'll try. I knew it was coming, too, but I thought we had some time. And by the way, you're pretty wonderful, yourself."

Steve laughed. "Thanks," he said. "And now there's one other thing I have to tell you. I've thought about this for a time and I don't want you to misunderstand what I'm going to say to you. I don't want you to sit around waiting for me to come back. I want you to be as happy as you can be while I'm gone. Date other guys if you like. I'll take my chances, but don't stay home and get the blues. I'm telling you this because I love you, and I don't want you to be unhappy."

Lisa was thinking of course she would be blue and unhappy. There would never be another man in her life like Steve. He had to be the best looking, the kindest and most wonderful man there was. "Let's not go out tonight," she said. "I want us to be alone tonight. I'll prepare supper here."

Steve laughed, "That's the best idea you've had lately. How about a glass of red wine?"

"You pour," Lisa suggested. She always liked to see Steve pour wine. He did it with such a flourish, throwing a large jug of wine over his shoulder and pouring into a glass he held in his left hand. It was so characteristic of Steve. She had seen him do it many times during the last years when friends were gathered at Steve and Jessica's apartment for Saturday night dinners.

It was after midnight when Steve left. Lisa was alone, and she knew that within a few days, Steve would be gone, and she would be alone without even the hope that he would be coming back soon.

There was a party the next evening at Steve and Jessica's garden apartment. Steve, as usual, poured the red wine and Jessica served Italian spaghetti and San Francisco sour dough bread. Jessica was a few years older than the University students who gathered at her apartment on Saturday evenings. Lisa often wondered why Jessica had never married. Probably in her mid thirties, Jessica seemed more like a chaperon than a participant in the gaiety that went on amongst the students. Tall, and statuesque, with soft brown eyes and short wavy brown hair, and a quietly commanding way about her, she tended to the needs of everyone. Lisa thought Jessica was one of the most wonderful people she had ever known, a very special person who always seemed to know how to make everybody happy. This evening, however, everyone felt like crying because they all knew that this would be the last party for a while. But no one cried. Instead they laughed and joked, and Lisa held back her tears, and laughed too. When the party was over Steve drove Lisa back to her apartment on Nob Hill. To Lisa's surprise he kissed her at the door, and did not enter the apartment. "It's too painful to say good-bye," he said, and he turned and left.

As Steve had predicted, he was accepted into the Army Air Force within a few days and was sent off to be trained as a pilot. Lisa never saw him again.

Lisa continued with her job as a publicity reporter, covering the sad tales of businessmen who were called to serve their country, leaving families and businesses behind. It was also distressing to say good-bye to the Japanese retailers along Grant Avenue, who were selling their wares at discount prices, leaving their stores, and reporting to the military authorities to be sent to internment camps for the duration. There was something tragic about their situation, and to Lisa it seemed unfair. The Americans of Japanese descent were loyal Americans who tried to tell everyone that they were anxious to fight on the U.S. side, but no-one would listen. At one point, the Japanese community at great expense and effort produced a play showing Japanese American men dressed in U.S. uniforms fighting against the Japanese military. Although numerous invitations were sent out to the public and the press, Lisa was the only non-Asian in attendance, and she was saddened.

It was a dreary time, and Lisa was restless. Steve was writing almost every day, but his letters were becoming restricted in detail and shorter. All she knew was that he was someplace in Alaska. Lisa was finding that letter-writing was no substitute for his company, but his letters helped to keep his image fresh in her mind. Steve had a zest for living and a spirit for adventure that, as a young man, had taken him around the world, working as a stevedore on cargo ships where he lived and worked with men as tough as himself. Steve was already a grown man with an unusual sense of responsibility when he entered the University of California to further his education. It was there that Steve and Lisa met and fell in love.

Steve was three years older than Lisa, and he had always seemed much more mature than the college boys who were his colleagues at the University of California. Steve and Lisa were freshmen when they met, and Lisa could never understand why he loved her. Steve was the kind of man every girl dreamed about, and Lisa knew that he could have had girls who were prettier, smarter, and more talented than she. Now Lisa missed him. Sometimes when she was alone in the apartment, Lisa deliberately tried to put Steve out of her mind because when she thought about him she would slip into a dark depression that was devastating. She had to keep trying to be happy, as she promised Steve she would. But it wasn't easy. Sometimes she feared that Steve might grow away from her and be different when he returned as a war hero. She feared that he might find that the girl he had left behind had become dull and unexciting. For some strange reason, the thought that he might not return never entered her mind.

At first, when the war fever ran high, Lisa didn't feel the loneliness so much because she and her girl friends were caught up in a social whirl of "going away to war" parties for young men who were being drafted or were enlisting. Finally, all who were left were the 4F's, the draft dodgers, and the married men with children. Lisa refused to enter into competition for the 4F's, was adamant in declining the propositions of the draft dodgers who wanted to "hide out" in her apartment, and she emphatically rejected the advances of the married men with children who had wives who didn't understand them.

There was no doubt about it, the action had passed her by, and Lisa was lonely.

It was December, 1942. Steve had been gone for almost a year, and Lisa no longer knew where he was, or what he was doing.

She was voicing her complaints to Geraldine, the office secretary, who was also grieving because her own fiance had been drafted.

"Everyone's leaving this city," Lisa said, "and if I knew where to go, I'd go too."

"Not everybody," Geraldine replied, "just the men."

"That's true," Lisa agreed. "We ought to do something about it."

"Like stop the war?"

"No, like getting a military job. Maybe we could be WACs or something."

"Geraldine shook her head. "I don't know about that. The pay isn't much and there's no security, and besides, I promised to wait."

"I'd be willing to sacrifice pay and security for a little excitement," Lisa said, and immediately felt a pang of guilt. If Geraldine could wait patiently, why was she so restless? Then she remembered that Steve had told her not to stay home and get the blues, and she knew she had to do something to make her life more meaningful.

"If action is what you want," Geraldine said, "here's an item in the paper that might interest you."

Lisa took the paper and read: "In the grey light of dawn, women wearing the dark grey uniform of the American Red Cross are quietly boarding troop ships, and sailing away to the war fronts with American GI's."

Methodically, Lisa folded the paper, laid it on the desk, picked up her purse and gloves, stood up, and said, "See you later, Geraldine. I'm off to enlist."

Lisa walked out of the San Francisco Examiner office, through the revolving outside door, on to Market Street where she caught a street car to Civic Center.

Lisa entered the old Civic Auditorium, made her way through ply-board petitioned war-time offices to the San Francisco area office of the American Red Cross where a motherly looking woman wearing the uniform of the American Red Cross greeted her, inquired her mission, and handed her an application form to fill out.

At that time, joining the American Red Cross was surprisingly easy. The personnel department was having difficulty filling its overseas commitments because private industry was offering higher salaries for war-time jobs than the Red Cross could afford to pay.

Almost anyone who could pass the basic requirement of a college degree or the "equivalent," and perhaps possessed some kind of talent or experience that would help the American Red Cross in its effort to improve the quality of life for U.S. soldiers overseas, would be hired. Lisa had the required college education, and could also play the piano, sing, dance and type.

When Lisa had completed the application papers, the motherly woman interviewed her for some five minutes concerning her reasons for wanting to join the American Red Cross. Lisa said she just wanted to help, and apparently that was enough. The woman handed her a medical form to be filled out by her family physician and returned as soon as possible. With that, Lisa was excused, and she stood up, shook hands with the woman and left the office.

Lisa caught a street car back to the Examiner office. On the way, she was pondering about the physical examination. She didn't have a family doctor because she had not been ill since graduation from college.

When she arrived at the Examiner building she noted the Phelan Building just across the street, and her problem was solved. Lisa walked across the street into the lobby of the Phelan Building and jotted down the office number of the first physician listed on the building directory.

The doctor was friendly and kind, and was also a patriot who agreed to conduct the examination and refused to accept payment.

Lisa returned to the Red Cross building and handed the physical examination form to the motherly American Red Cross woman.

"Is this all that is required?" she asked.

"That's all," the woman said with a smile. "You will be hearing from us soon."

Within two weeks Lisa received her first directive from the American Red Cross headquarters. The instructions were brief: "You will proceed immediately to American Red Cross headquarters in Washington D.C. for training."

Lisa submitted her resignation to the San Francisco Examiner, and agreed to help train a new girl who would take over her job.

Fortunately, Lisa's friend, Geraldine, was looking for an apartment at that time, and she agreed to sub-let Lisa's apartment for the duration and take care of Lisa's possessions until Lisa returned.

For the next few days Lisa was on the receiving end of farewell parties, saying good-bye to friends, relatives, and co-workers at the Examiner. Lisa felt no regrets except when she had to bid farewell to her widowed mother, Ethel

Medina, who lived across the bay in Oakland, and was a schoolteacher who had raised her three children alone. Lisa knew her Mom would be lonely, even though she would not say so. Lisa's brothers, Tom and Jim, had enlisted in the army and were in training, and now her mother's only daughter would also be gone. For the first time, Lisa noticed that her mother was getting old. In a few years she would retire from teaching. Her long dark hair was turning grey and there were lines across her forehead. Lisa was saddened when she saw her mother's eyes fill with tears when she kissed her daughter good-bye. It was one of the very few times that Lisa had seen her stoical mother weep.

CHAPTER 2

WASHINGTON D.C.

It was the week before Christmas, December, 1942, when Lisa boarded the cross-country train enroute to the National headquarters of the American Red Cross in Washington, D.C. where she reported for interviews with various executives of the national staff in one of the maze of huge government buildings there. The interviews lasted a full eight-hour day, and after they were over, Lisa was appointed as a "Staff Assistant," and was given a military rank which was equivalent to that of a captain in the army. The male interviewer explained that the rank applied only if she were captured by the enemy, in which case she would be treated as if she were a military officer.

"Captured by the enemy?" Lisa repeated after him. She was shocked because she had not once thought of that possibility, The interviewer, an elderly man with a kindly way about him, chuckled. "Don't worry," he said, "This is just in case such a thing might happen. There isn't much likelihood that it ever would."

Lisa was told that she would receive a monthly salary of one hundred and fifty dollars and would be expected to "full-fill whatever services or assignments that she might be asked to undertake by her superior officers." Lisa thought that was asking a lot, but she made no complaint.

The interviews were over, and the Red Cross interviewer handed Lisa a slip of paper on which he had written a room number at the luxurious Annapolis Hotel where she was to stay during the training course which would last for several weeks.

When Lisa knocked on the door at the Annapolis Hotel, it was opened by her new roommate, a young woman in Red Cross uniform whose name was Elsa Norris. Elsa was not what Lisa expected. Lisa's first thought was: "How can anyone look like Jean Harlowe in a Red Cross uniform?" Elsa's seductively curvaceous figure fitted into her uniform as if it had been poured there, topped off with shoulder length bleached blonde hair, sparkling blue-grey eyes, and perfectly shaped lips. Elsa looked like...well, she looked like what Lisa soon learned she was–a professional dancer and dancing instructoress, with a sexy appearance and a flirtatious smile.

"Welcome to this humble abode." Elsa said as she held out her hand in greeting.

"I've been in humbler places," Lisa answered. It was the beginning of a friendship that lasted a long time.

In the next few days it became apparent to Lisa that Elsa was uniquely equipped to get what she needed or wanted by a clever technique which she used to manipulate the male population. She would look a man directly in the eye and at the same time slightly shift her hips. It always amazed Lisa to watch strong men melt, and almost immediately acquiesce to whatever favor Elsa might be asking of them. Lisa also learned that Elsa was courageous, and in her own way, a loyal and patriotic American. But Elsa, Lisa soon learned, did not have the best disposition in the world. She was outspoken and critical, and sometimes hard to take. Nevertheless Lisa felt fortunate to be sharing a room with her. Elsa had already received several weeks of Red Cross training, and was ready to be shipped out. Also she had received her uniforms, and was the recipient of special favors from the hotel staff, and was commanding much curious attention from other guests in the hotel, especially from male members of the armed services. But for several days more, Lisa was still a nonentity, and went about her affairs unheralded and unacknowledged, until she too, received her uniform issue.

The American Red Cross furnished Lisa with two dark grey winter uniforms, one light grey overseas cap, and one dark grey winter overcoat. The rest of her clothing and equipment which included several pairs of black low-heeled walking shoes, luggage, military pocketbook, extra sweaters and blouses, and cotton underwear and stockings (silk or nylon, she was told, would be eaten by bugs in the tropics), were bought from her own funds.

Lisa was proud of her Red Cross uniform. She thought it was trim and practical, and during her three years of overseas service, she never tired of wearing it. As anyone who has ever worn a uniform knows, there is something about a uniform that sets one apart, brings attention, and is good for the ego.

The training program consisted of a series of lecture classes designed to acquaint the trainee with the history, development, ideals and purposes of the American Red Cross. The lectures, for the most part, were conducted by men and women who had spent many years in the Red Cross, and were quite capable of imbuing the trainees with an understanding of the Red Cross as a peace-time organization, but who were vague and obscure about war-time duties. That was because the staff didn't know any more than the trainees did about where overseas personnel would be sent, or what they were to do after they got there. Lisa understood that there was no way any human being could know what lay ahead. And later she understood that was just as well.

Although most of the lectures were of little practical value, one at least brought the classroom to attention. It was a lecture which was delivered by a woman physician, who they were told by trainees from previous classes, would talk about sex, because the Red Cross thought the girls should know the facts of life before being shipped to strange and foreign lands. But to the great disappointment of the class, the authorities must have changed their minds, or someone squealed on them, because the woman physician didn't talk about sex at all. Instead, she launched into a new topic with great enthusiasm. "How many of you," she asked, "have stocked up with physics?"

Lisa was one of the few who did not raise her hand, which was the right thing not to do, and she smiled smugly when the rest of the class squirmed as the woman physician charged them with a "Narcissus Complex," which, she said meant that they had never progressed past the "love-thyself" stage of life, and weren't even within shouting distance of the love-everybody stage, which is where she obviously thought they ought to be heading. Lisa was not sure about loving everybody. Her heart belonged to Steve, and to Lisa it seemed that would be forever so.

The doctor's parting advice was: "Your bowels are like Mary's little lamb. Leave them alone, and they'll come home."

All of this was interrupted by the advent of Christmas, 1942, when classes were dismissed for four days.

Christmas in Washington D.C. was more than anyone expected. Doors all over the city in private mansions, luxurious apartments, elegant hotels, and offices were flung open to welcome anyone who wore a uniform. Lisa was happy, and was enjoying a new and exciting adventure. At last she felt that she was a part of Steve's world, and would be doing her part in the war effort. The phone rang constantly, and Elsa and Lisa accepted invitations to dinners, dances, and parties with various escorts from the army, navy, and air forces. In between the festivities, there were guided tours to the Capitol, The White

House, Lincoln Memorial, Washington Monument, and The Smithsonian Museum. It was a wonderful time, and for some reason no one mentioned the war that everyone would soon be experiencing first-hand.

It was all over too soon, and Lisa was back in the headquarters building, and was attending class again.

There are landmark days in the lives of everyone...days that change the course of life forever. The first day of classes after the Christmas holiday was such a day for Lisa. After the first period, the lecturer asked Lisa to remain after class. Lisa was puzzled. Her first thought was that she must have failed in some respect. Instead, the instructor said, "I must caution you not to say anything to anyone about what I am going to tell you." Lisa nodded agreement.

"You are to be ready to leave Washington for New York Port of Embarkation by tomorrow morning."

"Tomorrow morning!" Lisa exclaimed. "I haven't bought any of the things I'm supposed to have."

"You will be excused for the rest of the classes today to shop for the supplies you will need overseas," he said as he handed her an envelope stamped "Secret Orders," which merely contained instructions to report to the New York Port of Embarkation.

Lisa put the envelope in her purse and left the room. Without even a last good-bye she lit out for the downtown stores where she bought everything she thought might be useful in the Sahara Desert or wherever in the world she might be sent. When she became overburdened with packages, she caught a taxi to the hotel, deposited the packages on the bed, and went downtown to buy more.

When the stores closed in her face, she continued to shop at cigar counters for extra combs, medical supplies, Kotex, and anything she could think of that might be scarce in the Sahara Desert.

When, at last, Lisa entered the hotel room that evening loaded with packages of goods that would be indispensable, Elsa met her at the door. "Where in the world have you been?" she asked. "Jessica has called twice. She said that she's Steve's sister, and she has important news of him, and she wants you to call her back."

A feeling of foreboding swept over Lisa as she laid the packages on the bed and reached for the telephone to dial the operator.

Jessica's voice was not reassuring. "Are you sitting down Lisa?"

"Yes."

"Steve's plane crashed last night... ran into a mountain in Alaska, and he won't be coming home."

There was silence. Lisa had stopped thinking. Finally, Jessica asked, "Are you all right Lisa?"

"Yes."Lisa answered softly. "I'll be coming home. You will need me."

"No," Jessica answered. "I knew you would say that. But I don't want you to come. I'll be all right. I want you to complete your mission...for Steve."

"I'll call you back," Lisa said. "I have to think."

"All right" Jessica said as she hung up the receiver.

Lisa lay down on the bed, and Elsa came over and sat down beside her. "It's Steve?" Elsa queried.

Lisa nodded. Elsa covered her with a quilt, and Lisa lay still while the God-given numbness that covers the mind and blanks out unbearable pain, spread over her like a comforting blanket.

After a bit, Lisa stood up and methodically, almost mechanically, began packing her suitcase and footlocker. Elsa watched anxiously. "She ought to be crying" Elsa mused. "Maybe she's gone out of her mind."

Almost as if reading her thoughts, Lisa said: "Don't worry, Elsa. I'll be all right."

In the short time following Jessica's call, not only had Lisa's dreams been shattered, but her commitment had changed. Jessica had told her what to do, and she would do it. She would complete her mission...for Steve. At that moment she became a dedicated servant of the American Red Cross on behalf of the men in uniform. The time for fun and games was over for Lisa.

Almost as if nothing had happened, Lisa spoke: "I have to be ready to leave for port of embarkation by tomorrow morning."

"Already?" Elsa asked in disbelief. "You haven't even started training."

Lisa shrugged, "I know."

Lisa picked up the phone to call Jessica. She had a message to import: "Jessica, we have to be brave... for Steve." It was a simple message, but Jessica understood.

"I know," Jessica answered. "God Speed"

Lisa and Elsa packed through most of the night, and the next morning they were sleepless, but ready. It was their first, but not their last, encounter with the army policy of "Hurry up and Wait." They didn't leave that morning, or the next, or the next. Instead they waited in Washington, and stocked up on army shots for every illness that was known to mankind, and they became acquainted with G-2.

Lisa knew that there were people who were spies, but it was new to her to be treated like a potential spy herself. She was always surprised when someone would click in on her telephone line and she knew G-2 was listening. And very often she thought she was being followed. This was disconcerting because she never really knew if she was being followed by G-2 or a masher. One morning a handsome young army officer stopped her as she was leaving the hotel to have breakfast at an adjoining lunch counter.

"You look nice in your uniform," he said pleasantly.

"Thank you" Lisa replied cautiously, wondering what he was up to.

"Are you glad to be going overseas?"he asked.

Lisa knew she wasn't supposed to answer that question, and was irritated with him for trying to trap her into saying something she wasn't supposed to say.

"If you're G-2," she said, "I wish you'd stop following me. You make me nervous, and I'm already fit to be hauled away by the man in the white coat."

"I know," he answered sympathetically, "but it's very important."

At the time, Lisa thought the military was carrying the spy-hunt too far, but only a few days later, she learned how important it was, and during the many months thereafter, she was glad G-2 was there.

CHAPTER 3

PORT OF EMBARKATION

Lisa and Elsa left the interesting and exciting life they had been leading in Washington, D.C.,with some regret when, along with some twenty-six other American Red Cross volunteers, they found themselves being transported before dawn via military vehicles to rooms at the St. George Hotel in Brooklyn, N.Y. where they were to await "further orders."

There must have been thousands upon thousands of soldiers who were processed for overseas duty through the New York Port of Embarkation. Perhaps they all suffered there as much as the young women of the American Red Cross who were drilled for hours across the icy docks, were taught to put on a gas mask to the count of three as they ran through a gas chamber, and then were sent to a photographer for a passport photo. This was particularly hard on Elsa. Her bleached hair had turned straight and stringy, her mascara had dripped from her lashes onto her cheeks, and her brilliant lipstick had faded away.

"Bitches," she complained. "At least they could have told us to bring a comb and make-up."

The passport photos were even worse than the girls thought they would be, and soon became a source of amusement for them as they competed for a prize for the worst one of all. To Elsa's consternation, she won hands down. "Bitches," she said.

The passport photos were attached to A.G.O. cards, and were the official if unrecognizable passports for the American Red Cross women into foreign lands, army P.X. stores, mess halls, and hospitals.

After the picture taking ordeal, the Red Cross girls were topped off with metal helmets, which were anything but flattering, and were issued metal dog tags stamped with their names and the name and address of nearest kin, which they were to wear around their necks in case they should be captured or killed. Then they were sent back to their rooms at the St. George Hotel. Altogether it had been a sobering ordeal.

The next morning before dawn, the Red Cross girls were ordered to make ready to set sail into the dark waters of the Atlantic Ocean.

Bundled into winter "woolies," woolen uniforms, winter overcoats, gabardine raincoats, overseas caps and helmets, and with musette bags, pocketbooks and gas masks hitched over their shoulders, and carrying suitcases which according to instructions from the liaison officer, were carefully packed with necessities to last at least a month, twenty eight Red Cross girls staggered out of the St. George Hotel via an underground servants' passageway which led into a narrow service alley.

There the girls found army trucks waiting for them, and Mr. Briggs, the Red Cross officer who had been assigned to shepherd the group to their destination, gave his first order: "Climb into the first truck until it's filled, and then fill the next one...and hurry!"

When the first truck was filled, Mr. Briggs closed the canvas back flap. "No one must see you on the way to the pier," he warned.

When the trucks arrived at the pier, the girls guessed immediately that they were headed for England instead of the Sahara Desert, because the dock was swarming with British sailors who watched curiously as Mr. Briggs called for the girls to "fall in" alongside the ship which loomed grey, grim, and formidable above them.

When the gangplank was lowered the girls climbed up, and as they reached the top, each one received a slip of paper from a British officer who was standing there. Across the paper was scribbled the number of a stateroom. Elsa turned to Lisa,"What's your number?"she asked.

"It's number seven."

Elsa hugged her. "Mine, too. We'll be together. I'm so glad."

Lisa was surprised at Elsa's obvious delight, but it made her feel good too. It was unusual that a capricious fate would place two people together who were as opposite as Lisa and Elsa. But for some reason, they seemed to compliment one another, and Lisa knew they would work well together in the mission they were undertaking.

The ship the girls boarded was H.M.S. Rangitata. It was a cargo liner belonging to the New Zealand Shipping Co. which in peacetime had been one of a fleet of ships that linked England with New Zealand and Australia. It was built to carry great quantities of meat, and for that reason, had been refrigerated throughout. The refrigeration had been turned off, but the overhead pipes which had been used for refrigeration continually dripped water. The former officers' staterooms had been turned over to the passengers, and were supposed to be heated, but for some reason the heating system was not working. For Elsa this caused great consternation. "I can't believe it," she said over and over again, "We'll all freeze."

"Maybe you won't freeze if you stop trying to show off your body," Lisa teased. "I intend to wear a sweater and coat day and night, and long woolies if I have to."

"Me, too," Elsa agreed. "Someone once said you have to keep the guys guessing, and they'll just have to guess about what kind of body I've got. I'm sure not going to freeze to make it easy for them."

The stateroom Lisa and Elsa shared with two other Red Cross girls was not much larger than a closet. It had one porthole which was "closed for the duration", four bunks, a wash bowl, and a doorway which was covered with a heavy black drape instead of a door to facilitate escape in case of emergency.

Lisa and Elsa deposited their gear on the bunks, and went back to the deck where they waved good-bye to well-wishing stevedores who were throwing apples to the passengers on deck.

It was not yet daylight when the Rangitata slipped out of New York harbor and headed into the dark waters of the open sea where German submarines lurked, waiting to attack Allied convoys.

But Lisa and Elsa were not thinking of the submarine war with the Germans. Their thoughts were of the land they were leaving behind, and they watched wistfully as the lights of New York City receded, and they wiped sentimental tears from their eyes when they passed the Statue of Liberty, bidding them farewell, instead of welcoming them to friendly American shores.

The Rangitata was returning to England from a trip around the Horn, and was carrying a diverse human cargo. There were civilians who had been stranded in British Territories by the war, and were returning home to England. There were British Merchant Marine men who had been rescued from sinking ships, and were reporting for re-assignment. There were Royal Air Force fliers who had completed a training course in the United States, and were returning to duty in the Royal Air Force. And there was a dashing corps of motorcycle troops from Canada.

The United States passengers included several hundred enlisted men who were under the command of an American army Major and were on their way to join the Allied Expeditionary Forces in England. And there were forty United States sailors who had already seen active duty on a U.S. submarine in the battle of Guadalcanal. They were under the command of a handsome young lieutenant, graduate of Annapolis, Lt. Larry Hanson. And there were twenty eight women of the American Red Cross, commanded by Mr. Briggs.

During the first day at sea, the Rangitata was joined by other ships to form a convoy.

Lisa had seen pictures of convoys in the newspapers. Always there were at least four destroyers and a battleship to fight off enemies, and numerous P.T. boats surrounding and protecting the troop carrier. But passengers on the Rangitata were not so fortunate. There were two corvettes (British version of a P.T. boat) and a destroyer in front and an oil tanker and two corvettes behind. That was all.

Lisa and Elsa and several other girls were on deck watching the ships line up. "I don't think we will look very threatening to the Germans," Lisa remarked.

"Maybe we can sail faster," Elsa replied.

Lisa shrugged. "I hope so."

And so the pitiful little convoy set sail on its voyage across the Atlantic Ocean.

CHAPTER 4

H.M.S. RANGITATA

The first day aboard the Rangitata was spent becoming acquainted with other passengers, and learning the routine of shipboard life. Mr. Briggs took command, and informed the Red Cross girls when and where they should go for meals in the dining room which was on the deck below, and ordered them to always be on time for their meal-time shift. He also warned them to accept orders from the ship's crew, and to obey all orders immediately.

Very soon God's eternal plan took over, and the Red Cross girls and various military men began to pair off for shipboard romances of one kind and another. This was an unexpected dilemma for Lisa, and she didn't know quite how to handle it. When a handsome young man from the Canadian motorcycle corps asked her to walk with him on the deck, she declined, saying she had other plans. It was a poor excuse, and Lisa was sorry. Later she confided to Elsa, and for the first time since she had learned of Steve's death, Lisa was weeping: "I just can't do it.I just can't."

Elsa was not sympathetic. "Of course you can," she said. "It's your duty to do what you can to make the military men happy; not make them feel rejected because of your grief over Steve. You don't have to sleep with them or even worse, marry them, just because they ask you to walk on the deck. It's part of your job."

Lisa dried her tears. She knew that Elsa was right, and she remembered Steve's wish for her. "Date other guys if you like. I want you to be happy."

Lisa vowed to do what she could to make life more pleasant for the men in uniform which, after all, was her American Red Cross mission.

The next day, Lt. Hanson, United States Navy, became Lisa's shipboard "date." He escorted her to the lounge for card games and an occasional after dinner gin and bitters. During the day they walked the deck, braving the icy winds of the North Atlantic Ocean, and they waved to the sailors on the tanker behind. In the evenings they sat huddled about a phony fireplace in the lounge. The logs were plastic, and the warm-looking glow was caused by an electric light bulb hidden underneath. It was, however, the only resemblance of heat aboard the Rangitata. The broken heating system was never repaired, and throughout the day and evening, the Red Cross girls all wore sweaters, overcoats, mittens and scarfs, and the bulky life preservers, which were called Mae Wests for obvious reasons.

Lt. Hanson was the perfect escort for Lisa. Always the gentleman, always attentive, always in command of every situation; he asked only for her time and companionship.

One afternoon, early in the trip, Lt. Hansen and Lisa were standing together at the rail on top deck, enjoying a bright sunny day which was a welcome change from the dismal cold of the past few days. Suddenly Lisa realized that she could be happy again. Just as clouds had drifted away to make way for the sun in the sky, the clouds had drifted out of Lisa's life, and she was warm and happy and the world was wonderful again.

"You're smiling,"Lt. Hanson noted.

"Yes. It's a beautiful day" Lisa replied.

It was, in fact, a day that marked a turning point in Lisa's life. Lisa wished that she could tell Lt. Hanson how much his kind attention had helped her, but she couldn't do that because Lt. Hanson didn't know about Steve, and would not have known what she was talking about. Lisa was sure that Steve, wherever he was, would be pleased to know that she could be happy again.

The Rangitata's British crew members deserved medals for service above and beyond the call of duty. In spite of incredible difficulties, they managed to preserve the "decencies" and customs of English life. The ship's Captain was never seen by the passengers. The British Liaison officer, an especially fine-looking and always proper young man who kept order and attended to the requirements of all passengers aboard, said that the Captain was always on duty at the helm, watching for enemy attacks on the ship and its human cargo.

All of the passengers were grateful, and tried to refrain from critical comments about the excessive cold, and deficiencies in the menu. All except Elsa, that is. Elsa was impatient with any kind of discomfort and she made it known that she didn't like the food, and she was totally unreasonable about the temperature.

"The British are doing this to us on purpose," she said. "They just want to save food and fuel."

And Elsa probably was right.The British were having terrible problems at that time trying to feed their own people from an almost barren cupboard, and to keep them from freezing because of a scarcity of coal. The addition of thousands of foreign soldiers and civilians who had to be kept reasonably warm and adequately fed must have been a nightmare. And the British people with their stiff upper-lip attitude, seemed to find it hard to admit that they couldn't cope.

On the very first morning Elsa's complaints went too far when she took out her ire on the room steward who brought hot tea to the stateroom. Lisa and the other two girls, Claire and Ann, were delighted when the curtains parted and the steward stepped inside with his tea-tray. But Elsa was outraged because she didn't like having her sleep interrupted. "Take that tea out of here at once" she commanded in a loud voice, "and don't come back."

The steward backed out quickly taking the tea tray with him. Lisa was speechless for a moment, too stunned to say anything. But she recovered quickly and for the first time gave Elsa a taste of her own medicine. "Well of all the selfish, self-centered people, you're the worst,"she said. "Maybe you don't like tea in the morning, but did it ever occur to you that we might?"

"Anyone who likes to drink tea before it's even daylight should have her head examined," Elsa grumbled.

Ann and Claire didn't say anything, probably because they were surprised by Elsa's outburst. But from that time on, through the entire trip, they barely spoke again to Elsa. Lisa was sorry because it was a bad start for their first day at sea.

Lisa was more forgiving than Anne and Claire because she knew more of Elsa's background. The fact of the matter was: Throughout her young life Elsa had been spoiled rotten by men. At an early age she had married an older and very wealthy and indulgent man who bought her a lovely home on the beach at Nassau, dressed her in glamorous clothes, sent her traveling about the world, and when she grew tired of it all, endowed her with a handsome divorce settlement. After that Elsa danced and flirted and used men as a means to relieve boredom and to furnish incessant pleasure. Lisa thought that there wasn't much left for Elsa to get excited about, and she wondered why Elsa had joined the American Red Cross in the first place. She should have known that she would be required to give up her luxurious life.

On board the Rangitata Elsa solved the problem of physical discomfort by staying in bed most of the day, wrapped in red ankle-length woolies, two sweaters, an overcoat and several layers of blankets pulled up around her chin until only her nose stuck out.

Elsa said it was too damned cold for any living human being, and she was quite right. It was.

But all that was boring and disagreeable to Elsa was wondrous and exciting to the other Red Cross girls, especially to Lisa. Lisa liked adventure, and was willing to sacrifice to become part of an exciting life. It was the reason she had chosen to become a newspaper woman, and it was her original reason for joining the overseas contingent of the American Red Cross. And now Lisa had become a dedicated person as well. She was determined to do her utmost to uphold the ideals of her American Red Cross obligation to help people in distress, and particularly the men in uniform who were fighting for their country. As Jessica had suggested, she was doing it for Steve.

It was a shock to Lisa when she discovered that not all of the Red Cross girls were so dedicated. Her first disillusionment occurred about 5:00 A.M. one morning while Elsa and Lisa were still asleep in their double bunk. Lisa was awakened by subdued voices just outside the doorway. She peered over the bunk and in the pre-dawn dimness, she saw a man's hand parting the curtain, and then his head appeared.Before she could say anything, another man appeared, and they were carrying another person.

There was something cockeyed here, and Lisa watched silently as the two men laid the body on the opposite lower bunk, and left without saying anything. For one horrified moment Lisa thought maybe someone had been murdered, but then the body groaned, and Lisa climbed down from her top bunk to look. It was Claire, and if she had been murdered it was a pleasant experience because she was smiling. Lisa was so absorbed with speculation of the situation that she hadn't noticed that Elsa and Ann were also awake and watching.

"Is she alive?" Elsa asked.

"Yes," Lisa answered, but maybe you'd better look at her.

Elsa climbed out of her bunk and peered into Claire's face. "For God's sake, Lisa, how can you be so naive? She's only drunk. Let's get back to bed."

"Ye Gods," Lisa exclaimed. "I wonder if anyone saw her. Isn't it awful for her to do a thing like this in uniform?"

"Well," Elsa answered cynically, "What do you expect of people?"

The incident had repercussions other than Lisa's disillusionment, and

Elsa's cynicism. Someone of the ship's crew had seen Claire being carried to her stateroom, and reported what he'd seen to the Captain who immediately issued stringent restrictions on all Red Cross personnel.

Red Cross girls were not to be seen below the officers' deck, and were not to speak to anyone below officer rank. The intimation was that the two men who carried Claire back to the stateroom were enlisted men. This entailed a double infraction of ship's rules which called for chastisement of those involved. But for the Red Cross girls this rule seemed unfair, and Lisa was disturbed. She felt it was her duty to do what she could to help the enlisted men as well as the officers.

Mr. Briggs was a quiet young man who disliked disturbances, and seemed somewhat at a loss as to how to handle his flock of females. "I don't like to be dictatorial," he said at the evening meeting after the "incident," "and I want you all to have as good a time as possible, but there is such a thing as discretion."

Mr. Briggs, however, agreed with the girls that they should pay some attention to the enlisted men aboard. Mild-mannered though he was, Mr. Briggs was persistent in his negotiations with the British brass, and he succeeded where many forceful characters have failed. He changed an Englishman's mind, and the Captain allowed the Red Cross girls to visit the enlisted mens' deck in an attempt to cheer the soldiers with amateur "song fests".The cast of entertainers in a song fest consisted of three or four Red Cross girl "singers" accompanied by a G.I. musician with a harmonica or accordion. It was a noble effort by Mr. Briggs, but was probably not worth the effort. Most of the G.I.'s were unimpressed, and some were obviously irritated because the amateur singing interrupted their card games.

However, some of the enlisted men were cordial, and sometimes they sang "Good Night, Ladies," when the girls left the deep, dark and dank enlisted mens' decks for the slightly more comfortable officers' quarters above.

Throughout the day, all passengers on the Rangitata were required to participate in precautionary measures in case of emergency. Everyone wore a Mae West at all times, and everyone cooperated for life boat drill. When the bell rang short continuous rings, all passengers were supposed to go to the emergency station on their own deck. When the bell rang one short and one long ring, they were to proceed to the top deck, and fall in for abandon-ship orders.

CHAPTER 5

U-BOATS

It was lunch time on Sunday, several days after the Rangitata had sailed out of New York Harbor. Lisa was enjoying the special lunch which the crew had prepared to mark a special day. Suddenly there was a loud crash which shook the Rangitata and sent dishes and cups skittering across the table. Lisa thought the ship had exploded. Although they had all been warned many times about the possibility of attack by German U-boats, Lisa did not think of that as a possibility. She had supposed that U-boats always sneaked up on ships that passed in the night. The idea of U-boats attacking in broad daylight, and on Sunday, did not occur to her.

The emergency bell started ringing short continuous rings, which meant passengers were to go to their emergency stations. Along with everyone else, Lisa stood up and was struggling to put on her overcoat and Mae West. Lt. Hanson came up behind her and calmly and politely helped her with her coat. Then with a quick salute, he was gone to attend to his duties as commander of the American Navy personnel on board. Lt. Hanson... a true hero, always an officer and a gentleman. Lisa was sure that he had been sent by a divine Providence to help her through the trying days after Steve's death.

At the time, however, Lisa was not thinking about how wonderful Lt. Hansen was. The ship's emergency bell was ringing short, continuous rings, and Lisa was trying to remember what that meant. Overwhelmed by the panic of the moment, she had forgotten! She was not concerned about that however, because by that time her instincts had taken over, and her instincts told her to get to the top deck and jump overboard.

She almost made it too. But when she reached the rail a guard grabbed her by the coat belt and collar and literally threw her down the stairs to the deck below. Subdued and ashamed, Lisa came to her senses and returned to her station where she found the other Red Cross personnel and Mr. Briggs calmly standing in the hallway holding their "escape kits." These were waterproof bags that were stocked with combs, lip-stick, towels, wash cloths, Kleenex, face cream and other things that might be useful in a lifeboat. Elsa, too, had braved the cold, and had crawled out of her bunk for this emergency. She was sitting on her escape kit, and she was laughing, which for some reason irritated Lisa. "What are you laughing about?" Lisa scolded. "It isn't funny."

"I'm laughing because everyone looks so scared. And besides it's better than crying."

" You have a weird sense of humor," Lisa remarked, and was immediately ashamed. "I'm sorry I said that. You did a lot better than I did."

Elsa laughed, "That's all right," I'm scared, too. I was worried about you. I thought you were never going to get here. Were you kissing Lt. Hanson a last farewell?"

"Not really," Lisa replied. "I was rescuing women and children."

"I really was worried about you,"Elsa said. "It would not be easy to break a new roommate in to my ways."

Lisa thought, "You can say that again." But she didn't say it, because she was proud of Elsa. Indeed, Elsa had the kind of courage that was an inspiration to Lisa. As she turned to enter the stateroom to pick up her escape kit, Lisa vowed to herself that she would never panic again, and all through the trying years ahead, she never did.

When Lisa returned from the stateroom, a Canadian officer was there briefing the group: "The Rangitata is not the ship that has been hit by a torpedo," he explained. "Although we were the main target, the first torpedo missed our ship and they took the tanker behind us."

"Is it sinking?" someone asked.

"It got a direct hit, and I doubt that it will make it to shore," the officer replied.

"Do you suppose we could see it?" Elsa asked, moving her hips and flashing her come-on smile which was her never- fail method of conning some man into doing something she wanted done.

"Yes, if you'd like." the officer replied, " I'll open the porthole in your stateroom, and you can see."

Lisa knew it was against regulations to open the porthole, and particularly in an emergency, and she started to so inform the officer. But Elsa put her hand over Lisa's mouth, and the officer opened the porthole.

Lisa and Elsa peered out and with startled and tear-filled eyes watched the drama of a sinking ship. The oil tanker had been hit dead center, and had caved in with both ends up, looking like a huge "V" for Victory sign. Heavy black smoke was billowing up around the ship, and the men who had often waved to them from the deck, were jumping over the side into the icy waters of the North Atlantic Sea.

Lisa watched anxiously, hoping to see a rescue ship pick up the men who were swimming about in the water. But all they could see was a Hudson bomber (probably from Iceland} which was flying overhead dropping depth charges into the ocean in an effort to strike and sink an enemy submarine. Lisa and Elsa were so engrossed in watching the tragedy unfold before them that they did not know an American officer was standing behind them until he yelled at them: "What do you two think you're doing?"

Both girls jumped away from the porthole and turned to face him. "We're watching," Elsa said inanely.

"That's obvious," the officer said sarcastically."I should report you for a reprimand. This isn't a game. This is war, and open portholes could cause deaths. Stupid! Stupid! Stupid!"

Lisa knew the officer was right, and once again she was ashamed for behaving badly in time of emergency.

But no-one could get away with calling Elsa stupid. "Go ahead, have us court-marshaled," she dared the officer. "that would be something different for the home folks to read about."

The officer glared at her, turned on his heel and left, and once again Lisa was witness to the awesome fact that Elsa knew almost everything about everything, and used her considerable knowledge to her own advantage.

Elsa knew, for instance, that the army couldn't do much about the Red Cross or its personnel. The Red Cross was an entity unto itself, and its members were protected by public opinion at home, a well-established but slow moving bureaucracy in Washington, and its own unique position as ombudsmen between the enlisted personnel and the military brass. The Red Cross people could, and sometimes did, get away with almost anything.

When the all-clear sounded, the Red Cross girls rushed to the top deck for a better view. By that time the stricken ship had stopped smoking, and miraculously was still afloat. They could see lifeboats catching the sunlight, bobbing about her. A corvette stayed with the ship, and they could see sprays of water shooting skyward whenever the Hudson bomber or the corvette dropped a depth charge. Lisa prayed: "Please God, save the seamen from drowning."

The Rangitata did not stop, but callously left the sinking ship and the convoy and headed south at full speed, zig zagging across the Atlantic Ocean... a maneuver which extended the length of the trip by some ten days. The food situation necessarily deteriorated, the temperature warmed and rumors ran rampant, such as: "The Rangitata was being followed, and had gone so far South it wouldn't reach England for weeks." The rumors didn't do anything to boost sagging morale, especially amongst the troops on the lower decks, who became moody and irritable. It was Mr. Briggs' idea to recruit Red Cross girls and enlisted men with any kind of talent, and organize a variety show to entertain the troops in an effort to relieve the deadly monotony.

Mr. Briggs expected the Red Cross personnel to contribute much of the talent, but he was disappointed. With the exception of Elsa, who was a professional dancer, and a girl called Mississippi, who had been a singer for a Mississippi Hill Billy band, he drew a dismal blank. However, all of the girls were willing to try, and they hoped to persuade Elsa to teach a chorus-line dance routine, but she refused. "I'll do a solo," she said.

Fortunately there was a really fabulous accordion musician aboard who agreed to furnish the music for whatever acts Mr. Briggs could come up with. Lisa decided to try out for a jitterbug routine. Her partner was a sailor by the name of Tom Brodier who was a phenomenal jitterbug. They won the try-out easily, and Tom set out to teach Lisa a professional routine.

After several days of six hours a day practice on a three-by-five foot platform at the head of a stairway, Lisa learned the rhythmic off-beat step of the jitterbug, and a dozen or more "wild" variations...a "rug-cutting" routine of kicks and whirls, and a fantastically difficult technique of cooperating while Tom whipped her between his legs and back on her feet. It was all quite impossible, but they did it.

During all this practice, Tom furnished the music, which was a mumbled and monotonous, but rhythmic, "Whatcha know, Joe. I don't know nothing."

When they danced in the show, the accordionist played "In the Mood," an inspired dance tune that would forever bring smiles to the faces of all jitterbug enthusiasts. Lisa was satisfied that she and Tom weren't bad, and in fact, they received an especially enthusiastic reception from the British and

Canadian forces aboard, most of whom were not acquainted with the jitterbug, which would soon become the most popular dance of the war years.

The star of the show was, of course, Elsa, who did a rhumba routine that was sexy and glamorous and showed off her astounding ability to twirl her hips about in a way that wowed the men. Elsa, who had some kind of a sixth sense, and was always prepared for any opportunity to shine over others, had brought with her a tight fitting black sequin dance dress, black nylon hose, and high-heeled shoes. Lisa thought Elsa's costume was unfair competition for the other Red Cross show girls who wore Red Cross uniforms and flat-heeled walking shoes.

Elsa's dance may have been a sensation, but most of the other acts in the show were good too, and some were show stoppers. There were singers, magicians, skits, and a group of six RAF flying sergeants, who had astonishingly well-trained and lovely voices, and who sang the wonderful Air Force songs; "I've Got Six Pence," and "Around the Square." Almost everyone agreed it was a fine show.

The only men who were not appreciative of the efforts of the variety show cast was a group of surly ex-guardhouse prisoners who were quartered in the meat freezing compartment on a lower deck. Surely, they had little cause to be happy about anything. They were to be among the first of the invasion forces, and that must have been an unpleasant prospect for the future. As for the present, they were crowded together, elbow to elbow, at long mess tables during the day, and at night they slept in hammocks which were swung above the tables. Day and night, refrigeration pipes dripped water on them. Perhaps they had a right to protest an invasion of their miserable quarters by more fortunate military personnel and a group of Red Cross girls who were trying to entertain them. Nevertheless, the cast members were disconcerted when the soldiers booed their efforts. Mr. Briggs soon cancelled the show, and directed the Red Cross girls to distribute comfort kits which contained playing cards, thread, needles, and buttons. Then he ordered the cast to leave the premises immediately.

During the long days, the American officers pulled rank, and amused themselves by ordering the Red Cross girls to report to the top deck where they commanded the girls to "fall in" for drill which included marching up smoke stacks, into life boats, and over the rail. Elsa was the only one who refused to submit herself to this indignity. When the order to top deck was relayed to her, she would merely grunt in disgust and turn over in her bunk. Nothing detrimental ever happened to her, and Lisa thought it must be wonderful to be as wise as Elsa.

Passengers aboard the Rangitata were always seeing things. Someone saw a flying fish; someone saw a whale; someone saw a school of porpoises; someone saw a human body. Then one day, someone saw a sea gull. And very soon thereafter they all saw land...Ireland. It was a wonderful sight for passengers aboard the Rangitata, and everyone rushed to the top deck to laugh, cry and applaud.

Soon, however, passengers were saddened when it came time to bid farewell to shipboard friends. The Rangitata docked at an Irish port, and that evening Lisa and Lt. Hanson were standing on deck watching a tender ship pull alongside when an officer came up to inform Lt. Hanson that he and his men were to board the tender within twenty minutes.

Lisa was shocked. "So soon?"

Lt. Hanson put his hand across her shoulder."Keep standing here," He said. "I want to see you once again before I leave." Then for the first time he put his arms around Lisa and kissed her on the lips. It was a tender, gentle kiss from a very young man who obviously had not kissed many girls in his young life before he became a Lieutenant in the U.S. Navy and was sent off to command an American submarine in the dangerous waters of the South Pacific. With a brisk salute he left to prepare his men to leave the ship. Lisa watched with tears in her eyes as Lt. Hanson and his men boarded the tender. Lt. Hanson then stood alone on the bow... straight, tall, and handsome. Wearing a navy uniform already decorated with medals for bravery in action, he stood at attention, saluting while the sailors sang "Anchor's Aweigh." Lisa waved until the tender disappeared in the dusk. She was thinking how much she was indebted to Lt. Hanson for helping to make her trip across the Atlantic a glorious adventure, and for the sailor, Tom Brodier, who taught her how to do a super jitterbug. She would never forget them. It did not enter her mind that she would never see them again.

The next day, the Rangitata sailed through the Irish Sea, and that evening docked at Avonmouth on the South coast of England. It was the last day of the twenty-two day voyage across the Atlantic Ocean, and the passengers danced on the deck, exchanged addresses with friends, and made plans to meet again in London. Mr. Briggs held an evening meeting which was attended by the British Liaison officer who had valiantly exerted strict control of the troops and civilians aboard the Rangitata. The Red Cross girls were pleasantly surprised when he complimented them for behaving "beautifully" and for bringing much cheer to the officers and men aboard the Rangitata.

Elsa couldn't control her glee. "We all thought you hated us," she taunted him.

"Of course not," he smiled. I thought you were wonderful, but it's my duty to appear stern to maintain discipline. I'm sorry."

Elsa smiled her sexy smile. "We forgive you," she said. "We think you are wonderful, too."

The officer's face turned red, and Lisa felt sorry for him.
She thought Elsa used her come-on tricks too much.

The other girls were irritated, too, and they glared at Elsa. The truth of the matter was that all of them were intrigued with this young Englishman who was handsome, disciplined, and who, all through the trip, had been completely unapproachable.

He had been the subject of many compliments and much speculation, and now Elsa was obviously attracting his attention. They were all just plain jealous.

The next morning dignitaries from Avonmouth came aboard the Rangitata to greet the passengers and welcome them to England. The Lord High Constable of Avonmouth was there in top hat and tails, and wearing a beautiful jeweled emblem about his neck. A British Air Commodore was there to greet the Canadian and British forces, and an American Major to greet the American forces.

The American Major called a meeting of the American personnel in the club room where he lectured them on how to conduct themselves in England. He warned them to observe security regulations, refrain from complaining about the accommodations or food, and he warned them not to mention Wally Windsor, whose marriage to Prince Edward had caused the prince to give up the throne of England.

The major then distributed booklets which reiterated all of his instructions except the Wally Windsor one, and also contained some valuable information about English money and its American equivalents.

After the lecture Mr. Briggs gave each girl a paper bag containing an apple and two meat sandwiches, and directed them to return to their staterooms and prepare to leave the ship.

"Mr. Briggs is a thoughtful man," Lisa remarked. "He even worries that we might not have enough to eat."

"He has been good to us." Elsa agreed. "At least he did the best he could under the circumstances."

The Red Cross girls donned their several layers of clothing, hitched their gas masks, musette bags, and pocketbooks over their shoulders, picked up their suitcases, and in full fighting regalia, marched down the gangplank, across the deck, and up to the English trains that were waiting there to receive them.

The English train was smaller than Lisa expected. "It looks like a Walt Disney cartoon train," she said. "I think it's kinda cute."

"I just hope it makes it to London," Elsa replied, as they settled themselves into a cramped compartment..

Elsa needn't have worried. The little train humped itself, jerked, groaned and puffed away without incident all the way to London Town where Mr. Briggs said they were to report to the American Red Cross headquarters and await further orders.

CHAPTER 6

LONDON

All along the way from Avonmouth, Lisa and Elsa looked for bomb damage, but to their surprise the countryside seemed peaceful and undamaged. It was not until the little train pulled into Paddington Station in London that they saw the dreadful effects of the war. The skeletons of great buildings were on all sides, dark, empty, blackened by smoke, their broken beams jagged and unlovely. Although the several blocks immediately surrounding Paddington Station were practically in ruin, the station itself was still standing, and as far as Lisa could see, was undamaged.

In full regalia, the Red Cross girls emerged from the train to face a crowd of curious English civilians who did not seem to know that there was a war going on in England. None of the English people wore helmets, and no one carried a gas mask! After their initial surprise, the Red Cross girls felt ridiculous. They knew that they were definitely overdressed!

Mr. Briggs, alone, remained undaunted. "Hup,"he shouted with military aplomb. The girls fell in, and with as much dignity as they could muster, marched across the station to the street where buses were waiting to take them to the American Red Cross Nurse's club at No. 10 Charles Street where they were to stay until they received further orders.

The Nurse's Club was probably the finest of all the Red Cross clubs in England. Its director was Mrs. Anthony Drexel Biddle, wife of the American ambassador to the exiled governments of Occupied Europe. Mrs. Biddle did a fantastic job of managing the Nurse's Club and dormitories, which in wartime England was not an easy accomplishment. It was said that she used great amounts of her own private funds to supplement Red Cross supplies. Mrs. Biddle certainly was a super "scrounger" and the food counters at the Nurses' Club were always laden with culinary delights that one could not find anyplace else in England. There was a cafeteria-style restaurant in the club where three hot meals were served daily, and there was also a brightly decorated snack bar where one could enjoy hors d'euvres, salads, and sweet rolls, and always hot coffee, coca-cola, fruit juices and hot cocoa. All of Mrs. Biddle's efforts were gratefully appreciated by the many American nurses, members of the American Red Cross, and the brave American women pilots who flew replacement planes across the Atlantic Ocean.

Lisa and Elsa and the other newly arrived Red Cross girls enjoyed a pleasant dinner, toured the club, marveled at how nice it was, and then lined up at the registration counter to be issued rooms in the dormitories across the street. Lisa and Elsa were assigned to a room with four others, and they all picked up their gear, and followed the doorman through the black-curtained maze which shielded the inside light from the outside, and stepped into the total darkness of blacked-out London.

It was their first experience with the English blackout, and Lisa thought it was eerie. Except for the muted lights of taxis that scurried through the streets, the blackness was complete. Now and then people brushed past on the sidewalk. The girls could feel and hear them, but could not see them. "It's scary" Lisa whispered.

"It sure is," Elsa whispered back. "A good place for a murder."

"You would think of something like that."

"Sorry, I can't help it if I'm weird," Elsa answered.

"I know," Lisa replied, "You were born that way."

Fortunately, they soon reached the dormitory and the doorman led them through another black-curtain maze into one of London's West End mansions, which had been converted into a dormitory to house American nurses and Red Cross personnel. All of the original furniture had been removed, and had been replaced with the bare essentials of dressers and cots. But the high ceilings and ornate woodwork revealed that originally it had been one of the fabulously luxurious homes of the English upper crust.

The room assigned to Lisa and Elsa and the other four girls was large, but its size was dwarfed by the bathroom, which must have held the square-footage record for all bathrooms in the world. It was carpeted with a red plush carpet and matching drapes hung at the ceiling to floor windows. At opposite corners of the room there was a huge wash bowl, and a lavatory that was perched on a pedestal with steps leading up to it. But most impressive of all was the bathtub which held court in the middle of the room, and was about four times the size of an ordinary bathtub. At the head it was equipped with a series of pipes running some seven feet high. Along the pipes were numerous knobs which turned hot and cold water into shower holes which were scattered about at various points along the pipes.

Lisa, overcome with curiosity, turned a knob at random. There was a great deal of gurgling, and the sound of running water, and suddenly a stream of water burst out of one of the pipes aimed at the drapes on the opposite side of the room. It failed in its destination only because Elsa was in the way. Frantically, Lisa turned knobs, trying to remember which one she had turned first, but she succeeded only in squirting more water across the room and drenching Elsa. Several girls ran to help, and they finally found the knob that turned the water off.

"Bitch," Elsa said.

The bath spout was a gold lion head with a ferocious mouth out of which warm water flowed peacefully and filled the enormous tub with enough warm water to swim in.

The girls took turns at the bath, their first fresh-water bath in almost a month. Then they climbed between the luxuriously clean sheets on their army cots and fell fast asleep.

Lisa was the first to awake in the morning. Being careful not to wake anyone, she slipped out of bed, tiptoed across the room and lifted the black-out curtains to see what kind of a day it was. It was a bright, sunny morning and she decided to take a walk before breakfast. She dressed quietly, and slipped out of the house.

Outside, Lisa turned right and walked past soot-grimed brick dwellings that were the pride of London's West End residents. At the end of the street, she came to London's famed Berkeley Square. There was a sign at the street corner which clearly read: "Berkeley Square," so she knew she was standing at the spot which had been the inspiration for one of her favorite songs. She marveled that a songwriter, even, could become so romantic about a dusty, vacant lot with a few tired trees and a shabby bench or two. As an unpatriotic Englishman wrote: "No self-respecting nightingale would have let out so much as a squawk within a hundred yards of the place."

Lisa sat down on one of the benches and tried to remember the verses of the song "A Nightingale Sang in Berkeley Square"

"That certain night, the night we met

There was magic abroad in the air

There were angels dining at the Ritz.
And a nightingale sang in Berkeley Square.
I may be right, I may be wrong
But I'm perfectly willing to swear
That when you turned and smiled at me
A nightingale sang in Berkeley Square..."

Before long, just like in the song, a young man came by, smiled at Lisa, and sat down beside her. But this man was not a dashing hero type. Rather, he was fairly nondescript...medium build, medium colored hair...medium everything. He was a man you would not notice in a crowd. "I understand that you are Lisa Medina," he said.

Lisa almost fell off the bench. "How do you know my name?" she inquired.

"I have been waiting for you to arrive," he explained. "I'm a friend of John Hammack, and he told me you were coming over, and to look you up."

"You mean John Hammack who owns a shop on Powell Street in San Francisco?"

"The same."

"I didn't know he knew I was joining the Red Cross. I haven't seen him since about a year ago when there was a fire at his place."

"I know. He was very grateful to you for the story you wrote, and he said I should do whatever I could for you."

Lisa was beginning to feel uncomfortable. She didn't know John Hammack that well. All she remembered was that he was an immigrant who owned a cosmopolitan dry goods store on Powell St., and when there was a fire which resulted in a big loss, she wrote a sympathetic story about how hard it was for an immigrant to start a business in a strange country. Lisa didn't know this young man at all, and she wondered about his interest in her. "By the way," she said. "I don't think I know your name."

"I'm sorry. My name is Harold Cross. I've been sent over to be a liaison officer between the army and the British, and between the army and organizations like the Red Cross. Some of my ancestors came from England, and I wanted to help. I haven't been assigned yet."

"I'm happy to meet you," Lisa said politely. But she was uneasy. There was something about this man that made her uncomfortable and she didn't know why.

Lisa stood up. "I must get back to the club," she said. "We are to have a briefing this morning."

Harold Cross stood and tipped his hat. "I understand. I'm sure we'll meet again."

Harold Cross was right. They would meet again. But there were no nightingales singing that morning in Berkeley Square, and clouds were forming in the sky, and the sun was gone. Lisa felt a sudden chill.

Lisa left quickly and returned to the club where she found the other girls already at breakfast, enjoying sweet rolls, coffee and the inevitable Red Cross doughnuts. Red Cross girls in England were nick- named "Doughnut Dollies" because they were always serving fresh doughnuts to the men in uniform wherever the troops were located...in England, in Europe, and even in Africa. Some ingenious soul had invented a doughnut making machine that was easily transported, and could almost immediately turn doughnut mixture into the finished product. The machines were quickly set up in Red Cross clubs and into vans, called clubmobiles, which brought the Red Cross girls and their doughnuts and fresh coffee directly to the front lines.

"I had a nice walk to Berkeley Square," Lisa said cheerfully, as she picked up a plate to serve herself at the breakfast buffet table.

"Oh, stop being so goody-goody-" Elsa said irritably.

Obviously Elsa hadn't as yet forgiven the shower incident of the night before.

After breakfast the girls left the club and caught a taxi to Red Cross headquarters in Grosvenor Square where Mr. Briggs had told them they were to be greeted by the American Red Cross Commissioner.

Lisa was intrigued with the London taxis and their drivers. The vehicles looked like flossed-up Model T Fords, equipped with double-jointed axles, that enabled them to turn themselves about in an area no larger than their chassis. But the taxis were no more incredible than their drivers, the youngest of whom were well past middle-age. They were invariably bearded, and sometimes gruff, and they drove their maneuverable little vehicles as if they did not fear the Devil himself. It was said that they drove about the London streets during the worst hours of the Blitz without paying any mind to the bombs and ack-ack that fell about them. The London taxi drivers, like so many other English civilians, were truly unsung heroes of the war.

Grosvenor Square was almost completely occupied by American forces, and the familiar Stars and Stripes flag was flying in front of almost every building on all four sides of the square.

The center of Grosvenor Square, which one could imagine was once a garden with flowers, green grass, and walks lined with benches where old men could sit in the sun and feed pigeons, was now completely militarized. The benches had been replaced by anti-aircraft guns which were camouflaged with bushes. In the center of the square, secured by strong cables, was a tremendous barrage balloon which sometimes nestled on the ground and sometimes floated in the sky above.

The barrage balloons, which floated all over London, were for protection of the city from low-flying German planes. The balloons and the cables kept enemy bombers high in the sky, and obscured special targets like the American Red Cross Headquarters in Grosvenor Square.

Lisa thought the barrage balloon was a good idea, and she didn't think it was funny when some disgruntled American soldiers joked that they would like to cut the balloon cables and let the British Island sink beneath the Sea.

The taxi driver brought his vehicle to a halt in front of a brick building where a large white flag with the Red Cross in the center, waved a welcome from above the door.

Lisa and Elsa and the other new members of the American Red Cross overseas force in England, trooped up a winding stairway, being careful not to step on the cleaning women who were on their hands and knees scrubbing down the stairs. Irrelevantly, Lisa thought that she had never seen anyone clean steps of public buildings in that manner in the United States.

At the top of the stairway, a photographer herded the group into a room where an American flag and a Red Cross flag were artistically arranged across one wall. The photographer arranged the girls in front of the flags, where they stood until the commissioner, Mr. Gibson, and his assistant, Mrs. Sloane Colt, arrived to have their pictures taken with the group.

If there were medals for members of the American Red Cross, Mr. Gibson and Mrs. Sloane Colt surely would have merited the highest that could be awarded. Those two cared for every one of their charges, no matter the problems which were numerous, unexpected, and difficult.

Fortunately the picture turned out to be an extremely flattering one of Lisa, and of Elsa, too. That was one other trick Elsa had learned. She knew how to pose for a flattering picture every time.

A flattering picture in this case proved to be important because while they waited in London for an assignment, Lisa and Elsa were often chosen to be invited to many special functions which were attended by dignitaries from all over the world. Lisa and Elsa were chosen to attend many of these affairs because they looked good in the official photograph.

The picture taking session was important too, because it was their first meeting with Mr. Gibson and Mrs. Colt, the two most important people in the London offices of the American Red Cross.

Mrs. Colt, particularly, was a friend to all of the Red Cross girls in England. A lady always, pretty and unassuming, she fulfilled her obligations as the official hostess for the American Red Cross, assistant to Mr. Gibson, and valued friend in need to the American Red Cross girls in England. During the following years, Mrs. Colt visited the lowliest at their stations, offering encouragement and badly needed help with their overwhelming problems.

Mr. Gibson described the various activities being undertaken by several divisions of the Red Cross. All divisions were in desperate need of personnel, so the Red Cross girls were told they could choose the type of work they preferred. There were three divisions open: Clubmobile, City Clubs, and Aero Clubs. The latter were clubs which were to be established for recreation on American air bases. The Aero Club was a new division, not yet in operation, and Mr. Gibson warned: "It is perhaps the most dangerous assignment, because American air fields are under attack from enemy planes. But it will also be the most exciting."

"That's for me." Elsa said immediately.

Lisa wasn't so sure, but by this time she was quite certain that Elsa knew more than she did about everything, so Lisa also joined the Aero Club division. And Elsa was right. It was exciting. Altogether, five girls in the group joined the aero club force.

Mr. Gibson directed the Aero Club girls to the office of Mr. Robert Allen, a young Southern gentleman, who was chief of Field Service. Mr. Allen was to have jurisdiction over the Aero Club Red Cross girls, who would be assigned to various air fields where they would report to a Red Cross field director on the base.

"I'm glad to welcome you into the Field Service," Mr. Allen greeted them. "I'm sorry to tell you that your stations have not yet been prepared, so you may take a few days off for sight-seeing. I'll call you when I need you."

"Whoops," Elsa said gleefully "That's wonderful. Now we can find a decent place to stay."

Lisa wasn't so happy about the situation. Being an Eager Beaver, she was anxious to get started helping the men in uniform.

Elsa began making plans. "We'll get a room at Claridges," she announced.

"That's all right with me," Lisa agreed. "One hotel is the same as another as far as I'm concerned."

Claridges, Lisa learned, was one of the most famous and also one of the most expensive hotels in the world. It was no wonder that Elsa knew about it.

"Thirty-five guineas a week for the least expensive of our double rooms," the room clerk said.

Lisa calculated quickly. "That's something like a hundred and forty dollars!" she exclaimed. "We can't afford it."

The clerk was understanding and helpful. "You might try the Mount Royal," he suggested.

The Mount Royal was a modern hotel, and looked clean and well-kept, so Lisa and Elsa rented a room there. It was a large and pleasant room. There were twin beds equipped with air filled mattresses, and satin down-filled comforters, down-filled pillows, and a modern tile bath...all for twenty four guineas a week. Lisa thought it was a great bargain, but Elsa had been used to far better accommodations, and did her best to bring the Mount Royal up to par.

One of the most pleasant of Elsa's habits was breakfasting in bed. Without any trouble at all, Lisa fell into the routine. Because Elsa was so much more efficient at directing service people than Lisa was, Elsa ordered breakfast every morning. The routine was always the same, but it never failed to intrigue Lisa. Elsa would pick up the phone from the stand by her bed. "Room service, please" she would say imperiously. Then, after a short wait: "This is room 1144. I am ordering breakfast for two. Prunes for two. Yes, I said prunes. I don't want herring. Prunes. Yes, Prunes! And scrambled eggs for two, if you can call that abomination scrambled eggs. A pot of coffee with milk, if you can call that limpid bilge milk. And now, please listen carefully and get this right. I'd like four slices of toast, buttered while still hot, and covered so that it will keep warm."

Apparently it was all very clear because then Elsa would hang up the receiver, and they would settle into their air mattresses and satin coverlets for an extra wink or two until there was a timid rap on the door announcing the maid with the breakfast tray.

For some reason the English people did not know that toast should be warm. The toast was always standing upright on a "toast rack" which guaranteed that it would be properly chilled on arrival.

When Elsa saw it she would shriek: "Take that toast back at once!"

The maid would meekly lay the tray on Elsa's bed saying apologetically, "I'm afraid this is the only way we serve toast."

"You see," Elsa would say to Lisa, "they hate us!"

Lisa's spirits were dimmed somewhat that very first day at the Mount Royal when she and Elsa entered the dining room for lunch. Harold Cross, the man she had met at Berkeley Square, was dining there with two other men. Harold Cross nodded and smiled at Lisa when she passed by his table, and Lisa nodded, but did not smile. The thought crossed her mind that he was following her, but she soon reasoned that it could not be so. He did not have time to learn where they were...or did he?

The "Hurry up and Wait" policy of the U.S. Army had extended to the American Red Cross. The few days Lisa and Elsa were promised before assignment turned into more than a week. Elsa filled her time dating and flirting with numerous men in the allied forces, while Lisa, like a wide-eyed school girl, wandered about London visiting historic sites.

Lisa and Elsa were never at a loss for escorts. London at that time was a whirlpool where military personnel from all the British services, and from almost every country in the world except Japan and Germany, milled about in pubs and hotels. There were French Canadians who had been the first to rush to the defense of English territory. There were Canadian fliers who came in droves to join the Royal Air Force. There were Australians and New Zealanders, Hindus, and Poles, dark-skinned Gibraltarians, French followers of De Gaulle, Representatives from China and hordes of Americans...all waiting for an opportunity to join the battle against the Axis, and all looking for a good time in London before their turn came.

Lisa and Elsa soon found themselves in the midst of a social whirl, rushing from one exciting event to another. During the first few days in

London Lisa was escorted by a young Canadian flying officer who was called "Brownie." Brownie had three days' leave in London before reporting to his station to begin missions as a fighter pilot with the Royal Air Force. Fortunately, the bombing of London by German planes, had ceased for the time being. The Blitz was over, and the "Little Blitz" had not yet started, and Lisa and Brownie made the most of favorable circumstances. They took photos of one another in front of the lion statues in Trafalgar Square, fed the pigeons there, and gazed with interest at the wax figures in Madam Tausaud's Wax Museum, noting that Wally Windsor was immortalized there along with the rest of the Royal Family. They visited Westminster Abbey where poets like Robert Burns and Robert Browning were lying under slabs beneath the floor, and others like old Chaucer tucked away in a niche in the wall. Each was a happy discovery for Lisa. They gazed at the altar where members of the Royal family were married, and where Kings and Queens were crowned, and they looked up at the Dome where workmen were repairing the damage done by a firebomb from a Nazi bomber.

The Royal tombs where Kings and Queens were buried were covered with sandbags that protected them from Nazi bombers and blocked them from view by visitors.

On the last day of Brownie's leave, he and Lisa visited the Houses of Parliament as the guests of Sir John Lucas, M.P. They saw Anthony Eden there, and Ernest Beven and were disappointed that Mr. Churchill was not there that day. In the evening they attended a dance at the Nurses' Club where they were entertained by Mr. Churchill's son-in-law, Vic Oliver. Then Brownie left, and Lisa never saw him again.

Elsa, during this time was involved with three British pilots who also were on leave before reporting to duty with the Royal Air Force. She danced with them, dined with them, and she rented a hotel room for them at the Mt. Royal, because she said, "They have no place to stay, and they don't have much money."

Lisa was curious. "Why are you so solicitous of these three?" she asked. "They aren't any different from all the rest, and you know you have a cold, cold heart where men are concerned."

"They haven't long to live," Elsa said quietly, "and I'm trying to make their last days as happy as I can."

"What a thing to say. How do you know they don't have long to live? Are you a prophet or something?"

"They'll be in the Royal Air Force soon, and they will be greatly outnumbered. They have to fly every day, and not many of them make it. They don't have much hope."

"I think it's wonderful of you to do that," Lisa said.

"It's the least I can do," Elsa answered.

Lisa was thinking of Brownie. He had said good-bye that very evening, saying he was reporting for duty with the Royal Air Force. It struck Lisa that he, too, would be flying against a superior force, and she was ashamed that she had not thought about the great danger he would be facing. She was comforted by the thought that she had told him to be sure and look her up on his first leave. He had promised he would do so. But now Lisa was not sure he could keep that promise. It was quite a jolt.

CHAPTER 7

RED CROSS AMBASSADORS

During the few days left before their assignments were ready, Lisa and Elsa were called upon to perform various ambassadorial duties on behalf of the American Red Cross headquarters. They attended dances and parties in honor of various people in England and from other countries who had benefitted the American Red Cross.

They had their photographs taken by a representative of the Associated Press as they distributed Junior Red Cross gift boxes to school children in a badly bombed section of Pimlico. They attended a fancy United Nations ball at the Mansion House as the guests of the Lord Mayor of London, where they danced with military and political representatives from all over the world.

Sometimes Lisa and Elsa found that their ambassadorial duties were not all that glamorous, but they knew that good will from all sources was important to the Red Cross, so they participated as well as they could. One evening they agreed to accompany the American Red Cross personnel director to a dinner party at the ritzy Ambassador Hotel which was hosted by several English businessmen who had been instrumental in establishing the American Red Cross in England. Lisa felt awkward and uncomfortable dining and dancing in a public place with six men, but Elsa didn't seem to mind. Elsa was actually having a good time because one of the gentlemen was an excellent rhumba dancer, and even though he was several inches shorter and some years older than Elsa, they put on quite a show. Some of the other dancers even stopped dancing to applaud, which of course was music to Elsa's ears.

Lisa, who was left to dance with the other five men in turn, was not so fortunate. They were all older gentlemen, and there was not a particularly good dancer in the group, and certainly none who could do the jitterbug. And there was another reason that caused Lisa to hope for an early end to the evening. At a table on the edge of the dance floor she saw Harold Cross dining with the same two men she had seen with him at the Mount Royal Hotel on her first night there. This time, however, Harold Cross was wearing the uniform of the United States Air Force. When Lisa danced past his table, she turned her head, and did not speak, and she wondered why she felt so strongly apprehensive of this man. It was a compulsion she could not explain. Lisa was glad when the gentlemen who were hosting the party, suggested that the group leave the Dorchester and finish the evening at a "Bottle Club" in the Soho district.

Bottle Clubs thrived in London because it was illegal to serve liquor in a restaurant or pub after midnight. So, for the purpose of preventing many a well-started party from breaking up too soon, enterprising Englishmen established "clubs" and sold memberships to anyone who was willing to pay premium prices for liquor and entertainment.

When the group arrived at the Bottle Club, a floor show was in progress, the lights were dim, and they were led to a secluded table where they were joined by several hostesses who worked there encouraging men to purchase more champagne than they otherwise might. At that point the Red Cross personnel director stood up to excuse himself and the Red Cross girls, saying he had an obligation to return his charges at a "reasonable" hour.

Elsa complained, "The party's just getting good." But Elsa obediently stood up, and her dancing partner arose to help her obtain her coat at the check-out counter.

Lisa stood up also, and trying to be polite, addressed her hosts: "I thank you for this very extravagant and interesting evening."

"My dear girl," one of the gentlemen answered as he stood with the others. "We're not being extravagant, we're spending excess profits which otherwise would be taken away in taxes."

The next evening Lisa and Elsa were scheduled to a far different affair. A very wealthy English socialite by the name of Jane Ellsworth, who called herself a Marxist Socialist, invited Lisa and Elsa and two American Red Cross men to tour London's East End slum district. The first visit of the evening was a play shelter in a school where late-working parents left their children until they returned home from work. The children appeared poor indeed. They were thin and looked underfed, and the school room was chilly and bleak.

When the group left the school, darkness was descending, and the air was cold and damp, and Lisa noticed a little girl, perhaps some eight years of age, limping along the sidewalk ahead. "Why is she limping?" Lisa asked.

"She limps because she has chillblains," Jane explained. "And she has chillblains because her mother can't afford to buy coal or proper clothing for her children."

Next the group stopped to have a cup of tea at the home of an East End resident who was an acquaintance of Joan. It was an abject place, but the woman of the house was plump and friendly, and immediately cleared the table of papers, sewing materials, and dirty dishes, and began preparing tea. Her young daughter, who worked as a hostess at a bottle club, was there, too. She was a pretty girl, and she watched quietly as she sipped tea, and cupped her hands around the tea mug for warmth.

Joan was lecturing as usual, proclaiming the injustices of the social system in England. "Poverty like this," she said, "is the fault of the rich people in the West End. Off with their heads!"

Lisa was wondering if Joan, who lived in the West End and was rich, included herself as one of those who warranted beheading.

The young night club hostess must have had a similar thought, and she spoke for the first time: "I'd as soon a West End bloke bought me a pint, as a bloke from the Ministry of Labour."

The next stop was an East End air raid shelter, and it too, was bleak. Actually, it was a terrible place. Consisting of a series of large, concrete holes in the ground, connected with the outside, and with each other by narrow tunnels, it was damp, depressing, and it smelled terrible. It was crowded with wrinkled, toothless old men and women who lay about on sagging bunks.

A grumpy middle-aged woman seemed to be in charge, and she obviously didn't want to be bothered with visitors, and told them so. "I been keepin' these digs all through this war", she said, "and I won't be puttin' up with this, I won't!"

Lisa was startled and a little frightened. "Let's get out of here," she said to Jane.

Jane tried her best to calm the manageress with no success, so they all left the premises without further ado. Lisa vowed that she would never enter an air raid shelter again, no matter what, and she never did.

It was Jane's idea that they should end the evening with dinner in the celebrated Soho district of restaurants, pubs, and bottle clubs where

Bohemians gathered for talk, food, and drink...wherever they could find someone willing to pick up the tab.

Jane guided the group along the blacked-out sidewalks, in and out of black-curtained mazes and shabby pubs where patrons in worn "civies" and soldiers in uniform were served by beer-stained bartenders crowded around cluttered tables talking all at once.

At one of the pubs, Jane introduced some special friends of hers, including a Hindu writer whose name was Annan, and who Jane said was married to a beautiful blonde English girl, and was the father of a little blue-eyed baby girl. Annan's hair was long and dark, and curled slightly at the ends. He wore a long, vari-colored silk tie that wound about his neck, tied in a dashing bow at this throat, and fell down to his knees. Annan was obviously dressed to attract attention, so Lisa ventured a remark about his attire. Annan was happy to reply: "Amongst the people I know," he explained, "I can wear bright colors, huge ties, and long hair with impunity." As more of Jane's friends gathered around the table, Lisa had to agree that anybody could wear anything with impunity in this group. Lisa felt very drab in her Red Cross uniform.

Before long someone suggested that they should go to the Hong Kong restaurant for a "bite." The bite that had been suggested turned out to be a feast. Each person in the group knew a particular dish for which this restaurant was renowned, and each ordered his dish "all around." The table was stacked with really delicious food.

Throughout the dinner Jane often raised her glass to propose a toast. It was always the same: "Off with their Heads!"

The Red Cross men should have been particularly impressed with it all, because they paid the bill. Lisa was outraged, because she knew that all Red Cross personnel were on very limited salaries, including the men. She quietly remonstrated to one of them. "Why don't you let Jane pick up the tab? These are all friends of hers, and besides she's rich. Off with her head!"

But the Red Cross men were gentlemen at all costs, and even refused Lisa's and Elsa's offers to share the bill. "I think there's a lot of hypocrisy with these rich Marxist Socialists," Lisa remarked as they left the restaurant.

"You're right about that" Elsa agreed, "but what can you expect of people?"

Elsa's cynicism about people did not extend to the American Red Cross assistant director, Mrs. Sloane Colt, an American socialite who took her responsibility towards her Red Cross charges seriously. Mrs. Colt even wrote a note to Lisa and Elsa suggesting that they move to a "safer" hotel, which was a surprise to them because they thought they were safe where they were. Mrs. Colt also worried that the Red Cross girls were not warm enough in their American-made uniforms, so she obtained clothing coupons from the English government, and sent all of the Red Cross girls to an exclusive London tailor to be fitted for Royal Air Force blue uniforms and matching overcoats with red linings.

Lisa and Elsa were delighted, and Elsa expressed her appreciation: "Mrs. Colt is one of the finest people I've ever known," she said.

"I agree," Lisa answered.

CHAPTER 8

AERO CLUB ASSIGNMENT

All good things must come to an end, and for the aero club volunteers that time had come. It was time for them to pick up their shovels and start shoveling, and it must be said that Lisa and Elsa did not falter.

No one could have anticipated the problems facing the Red Cross Aero Club directors. Probably this was just as well because if the volunteers had known what they would be up against, they would not have volunteered. Lisa and Elsa were fortunate because, as they learned from later reports, their problems were not as severe as those faced by others in the group. A few months later, some of the girls had to be sent back to the States tagged "mental exhaustion," and Dr. McDonald, the official Red Cross physician who attended them, complained about the intolerable conditions to which they had been subjected.

It was a cold, dark day in London when Lisa and Elsa made their way to the headquarters office where Mr. Frank Allen was to brief them on their new mission. Lisa and Elsa and the three other Aero Club volunteers stood before Mr. Allen's desk, awaiting instructions relative to their new assignments.

Mr. Allen apparently believed in the hypothesis that ignorance is bliss, because he certainly didn't reveal any information about what Aero Club Directors were supposed to do. Lisa and Elsa and the others tumbled all over themselves asking questions; What do aero clubs look like? Where will we live? Will we have help? How do we pay for help? Where will we obtain food? Mr. Allen dodged all their questions. Finally the girls fell quiet and waited.

Mr. Allen rummaged about in his desk, and finally produced five stop watches, the kind that are used for field meets, swimming contests, etc. Solemnly, he handed one to each of the girls. "Keep these carefully," he said. "They're very hard to get over here."

The girls turned the watches about in their hands, wondering what they were supposed to do with them, but none dared ask, and Mr. Allen did not enlighten them.

Almost as if it were an afterthought, Mr. Allen opened a desk drawer and said; "Oh yes, you all have mail here from the United States."

That statement brought the girls to attention. Mail from home! Nothing can match the excitement of letters from home for anyone who has been on a foreign shore during time of war.

Lisa had a letter from Jessica, reporting about the military funeral that was held in Berkeley for Steve. It was a short note, and comforting for Lisa: "I'm so proud of you, Lisa, I know Steve is too. Nothing you ever could have done, would have pleased him more than what you're doing."

There also was a letter from her mother and many others from friends... all offering good wishes and encouragement.

Elsa, too, was pleased with the letters she received, mostly from men she knew who had written from various places around the country, wishing her well and exacting promises from her to meet them again after the war. Elsa couldn't help gloating.

Then Mr. Allen distributed five copies of a month old Saturday Evening Post and with a flourish that would have done credit to his Southern ancestors, he presented each girl with two flags. One was the Stars and Stripes, and the other was the emblem of the American Red Cross.

"Is that all?" someone asked.

"That's all" Mr. Allen answered, "except...Good Luck!"

As they filed out of the office, equipped with everything they would need in any eventuality, Mr. Allen's secretary handed each girl a sealed envelope. Inside was a slip of paper on which was typed the name of the city nearest the American airfield where they were to be stationed, and the departure hour of the train that would take them there.

Elsa and Lisa were to take the same train to Bury St. Edmunds in Suffolk County, and were to report to the same field director, Michael Stutz, who would meet them at the train depot.

The train left at 2;00 P.M. and as it was then only 11:00 A.M., the girls thought they would have time to pick up their luggage at the hotel, and have time for lunch. But they didn't reckon with the necessity of adding an hour to every schedule made in England. Lisa and Elsa were already late and in danger of missing their train, when they finally flagged a taxi, and explained their need for a speedy ride to Liverpool Station. The driver took off, and as the girls bounced about in the back seat, they thanked the Good Lord for the London taxi drivers who were the only beings capable of hurrying in all of England.

They caught the train just in time. Their luggage, which they had entrusted to a porter with a little cart, did not do so well. As they scrambled aboard the train which was already beginning to move, the porter, in front of their horrified eyes, came ambling along the walkway with their luggage still in his cart. He seemed completely unconcerned that he had not a chance of getting the luggage on the train.

Quick-on-the-trigger Elsa called to him and threw some shillings on the ground at his feet. "Send our luggage to Bury St. Edmunds on the next train," she called.

The train, like all trains in England at that time, was crowded to capacity, but Lisa and Elsa wedged themselves into an already overflowing compartment where they sat sideways between English civilians, soldiers, and Land Army girls.

Lisa and Elsa were quiet most of the way to Bury St. Edmunds. They were worrying about their luggage, and they were tired and apprehensive about what lay ahead. They had not managed a very good start on their new assignment.

Lisa expressed her disappointment. "It's been almost two months since we joined the Red Cross, and so far we haven't been of much use."

"I wouldn't say that," Elsa objected. "After all, we've been through training, we've been fitted with uniforms, shipped half-way around the world, have had a week's vacation, and have lost all our worldly possessions to the cause. I don't call that so bad."

"It seems like such a long time," Lisa mused. "We should have been working weeks ago."

"I wouldn't be too anxious if I were you," Elsa said with uncanny foresight.

Lisa sat through most of the trip gazing out of the window and seeing nothing. She was trying to envision what the club would be like. She pictured a cozy road-house with dimmed lights, a juke box perhaps, and a small dance floor where G.I.'s could bring their dates and have a pleasant evening away from the routine of the Army. She was so engrossed with her thoughts that she didn't even notice when they passed through Cambridge of University fame and Newmarket of turf fame. It was after 7;00 P.M. when they reached Bury St. Edmunds, and already too dark to see anything until the train came to a stand-still at the station platform, and then Lisa got a shock she wouldn't soon forget. There on the platform waiting for them was Harold Cross.

"How do you do, Miss Medina," he greeted her.

"What are you doing here?" Lisa enquired, too upset to be polite.

Elsa was surprised. "Do you two know each other?

"Yes," Lisa said, "We've met before. This is Elsa Norris, meet Harold Cross."

Harold Cross nodded. "I've been assigned to the airfield here," he explained. "Your field director, Mickey Stutz, has been called away on an emergency, and he asked me to meet you and take you to a hotel. Where are your bags?"

Elsa explained that the bags would be on the next train, and Harold Cross obligingly said, "We'll pick them up in the morning. They'll be stored for you. The British are very good about things like that."

"All right, where do we go from here?" Elsa asked.

Harold Cross hesitated. "I don't like to tell you this," he said, "but Mickey forgot to book a room for you. I tried to find something, but the only place available isn't too good. I hope you won't mind."

Lisa was uneasy. What did Harold Cross mean by "not too good?"

Lisa was soon to find out. Harold Cross had a jeep waiting downstairs on the street, and the G.I. driver took them to an old Inn that Shakespeare might have described as a "public house, haunted by the ghosts of rake and strumpet who had gone before." But Lisa and Elsa, being Americans, and not so flowery, described it as a tumble-down dive. And that it surely was.

The Innkeeper who doubled as a bartender in a noisy and disreputable pub on the first floor, came to the door in answer to Harold's knock.

"Hello Jerry," Harold said.

"Welcome, Harold."

Lisa was surprised. Obviously Harold knew this man, and that seemed odd. The innkeeper was not the kind of man Lisa thought Harold would be associating with. Entirely in keeping with his establishment, he was dirty and malevolent looking, and from a toothless cavern of a mouth he mumbled that the room was upstairs.

"The room" contained a double bed which had seen better days, and was bumpy and gnarled looking. It was the only piece of furniture in the room. "Before the war." the inn-keeper said, "there was windows, too, but the blast from a bomb knocked 'em out. Close bugger, that 'un."

Elsa was appalled. "We can't stay in a place like this." she said.

"We'll take it," Lisa chimed in. "We're tired and we need some rest."

After Harold and Jerry left, Elsa asked the question that had been bothering her.

"Where in the world did you find a couple of weirdos like these?"

"I didn't find them," Lisa answered irritably. "They found me, and don't ask me why, because I don't know."

"Maybe they're spies, or something."

"Why would you say a thing like that? If they're spies, why would they be interested in us? We don't know anything about anything."

"Maybe they think we do."

"I'm going to bed. I'm tired." Lisa said.

That night, exhausted though they were, the girls found it was almost impossible to sleep. They tossed and turned, and bumped into one another in bed until the early hours of morning when they finally dozed off, succumbing at last to an exhaustion that won the battle against broken bed springs which jabbed into them, crawly things that crept over their bodies, and rowdy noises from the pub below.

Elsa was the first to arise. It was probably the only time in her life she had ever been first out of bed, but this morning she had an important mission to accomplish. "I," she said, "am going to find a room with windows and heat."

With the help of a friendly hotel keeper, Elsa accomplished her mission. By noon she and Lisa were cozily toasting their toes before a six-pence-devouring gas heater at the Angel Hotel. To Lisa and Elsa the Angel Hotel was all that its name implied. There were two wonderfully comfortable beds with goose-down comforters and clean sheets, and there were windows with glass in them. Down the hall was a W.C. (Water Closet) and a bathroom. The bathroom, however, was always locked except on Fridays, when everyone who was staying at the hotel was supposed to bathe. Not even Elsa could wheedle her way in on any other day, although she tried.

Lisa did not complain about the bathroom inconvenience. Rather, she was intrigued and delighted because the bath was historic. The manageress said it was the very same bath Charles Dickens used when he lived at the Angel Hotel. The manageress also said that Dickens wrote in his Pickwick Papers about Mr. Pickwick and Sam Weller visiting the Angel Hotel where Mr. Pickwick "had a very satisfactory dinner," and where Sam Weller used the pump in the yard for his ablutions, and where they were both victimized by Alfred Jingle.

Elsa couldn't resist: "Did Sam Weller use the pump in the yard because the bath was locked then?"

Without answering, the manageress turned to leave the room.

But Elsa got in a last crack: "Well, at least we haven't been victimized... yet."

The first day at the Angel Hotel was a Landmark day for Elsa Norris and Lisa Medina. It was a day that would change their lives forever...a magic day, when anything at all could happen...and did. It all started when they entered the dining room for lunch and were seated by the maitre'd near a table that was occupied by two American air force officers.

The waiter who came to their table, informed Lisa and Elsa that the gentlemen at the next table would like to buy a drink for them. Lisa and Elsa smiled at the officers, and nodded agreement, and that started it all. The next step of course, the officers asked permission to join Lisa and Elsa at their table, and Lisa and Elsa welcomed them.

The officers introduced themselves...Lt. Larry Aronson and Lt. Andy Thompson, and they shook hands with Lisa and Elsa. It was all very proper.

Lisa and Elsa soon learned that Lt. Aronson and Lt. Thompson were air force pilots in a bomb group which was stationed several miles out of Bury St. Edmunds. The base was not yet in operation. In the meantime, the crews and pilots were waiting, and doing what they could to entertain themselves in the little village of Bury St. Edmunds.

Lisa and Elsa were extremely interested because they were anxious to know about the base and their duties there. Lisa wondered aloud: "Do you suppose that's where we will be stationed? We're Aero Club directors, and we're supposed to establish an aero club around here some place."

Lt. Thompson spoke to Lisa. "I sure hope you'll be at our base."

Lt. Aronson spoke to Elsa. "I hope you'll be stationed at our base, also."

The couples had just finished what they all agreed was a very pleasant lunch, even though the menu was less than satisfactory, consisting of mealy sausages which were more cereal than meat, soggy potatoes, and butterless rolls. They were leaving the dining room when Lisa saw Harold Cross and Michael (Mickey) Stutz, the American Red Cross field director, entering the hotel lobby. Mickey Stutz was a large man with a slightly rumpled appearance, even in uniform. His ash-brown hair refused to stay in place, and he looked like he needed a shave. Mickey and Harold spoke to Lt Aronson and Lt. Thompson without introduction, so the girls knew that they were acquainted. Then Mickey smiled a friendly smile, as he shook hands with Lisa and Elsa in greeting, asking each girl's name as he did so. "I'm glad you're here" he said. " the NAAFI left last week, and the G.I.'S are getting impatient for a replacement."

"What's the NAAFI?" Elsa asked.

"NAAFI is short for National Army Air Force Institute. They do for the British airmen what the Red Cross does for the Americans. They were on the base when we arrived because it was an RAF base before we came. They're better organized than we are, and they have better access to food and furniture supplies than we have. The enlisted men are upset that we let the NAAFI go. But don't let it bother you. They'll get over it when they see what we can do."

"What can we do?" Elsa asked.

"That's your job," Mickey replied. "Now we have to draw straws."

"Draw straws?" Lisa exclaimed. "What for?"

"To decide who gets the station nearest town," Mickey answered, as if he were talking sense.

"You mean Elsa and I are to be at different stations?"

"That's right," Mickey said. "You will each have a club of your own. Didn't you know?"

Elsa entered the conversation. "No," she snapped. "We didn't know. But that's nothing new. We don't know anything. We're too stupid to know anything. Only the geniuses at headquarters know anything, and they aren't talking."

"It's not that bad," Lisa said, hoping to calm Elsa down, but it was no use.

"Oh stop the Polly Anna stuff. I can't stand that anytime, and especially now."

"All right. All right. Lisa said. "I suppose we'd better draw straws."

"Yes, to be sure," Mickey said as he thrust out his fist with the two straws between his forefinger and thumb. "I have them ready. Lisa will pull one out and Elsa will take the one that's left. The long one will go to the nearest and largest base, and the short one will go to the base out in the sticks."

Lisa drew the long straw for the nearest and largest station.

"That's fine," Elsa exclaimed in exasperation, "There isn't anything I would like better than to be stationed alone out in the sticks. But first, maybe we'd better go to the station and pick up our luggage. I don't want to be out in the sticks without any clothes."

Lt. Aronson and Lt. Thompson who had been politely silent through it all, broke into laughter. "Would you want us to go with you?" Lt. Aronson asked. "I'm good at carrying luggage."

Elsa turned and smiled at him, and Lisa knew that the crisis was over for the time being. Lisa was thinking that Lt. Aronson would be good for Elsa. They made a fine pair. Lt. Aronson had blonde curly hair, and a winning smile and he used his good looks to attract members of the opposite sex, just as Elsa used her beauty to do the same thing. If one wanted to be catty, one would have to say that Lt. Aronson was a real blonde and Elsa was a bleached blonde, but the effect was the same. On the way to the station Lisa was hoping that the luggage would have safely arrived, but she was disappointed. "Your luggage should be here within three days," the station master said.

"You see," Elsa said. "They hate us."

After the group arrived back at the hotel, Mickey and Harold Cross said they had to leave. "I'll pick you up first thing in the morning," Mickey said. "You'll be staying at your stations tomorrow night."

Lisa was apprehensive. Things didn't seem to be going as they should, and Mickey didn't seem to care. After Mickey and Harold left, Lisa turned to Lt. Thompson. "Will I be at the base where you are?"

"Yes," he answered.

"Are there many airmen stationed there?"

"Several thousand."

"And women?"

Lt. Thompson grinned. "No women. Just you."

"I'll be lonely."

Lt. Thompson put his arm around her shoulder. "No, I'll be coming to see you."

Elsa broke into the conversation, "And I'll be alone out in the sticks?"

"No," Lt. Aronson said, "I'll be coming to see you."

Elsa smiled, and Lisa marveled that Lt. Aronson could bring Elsa out of a mood so quickly.

Lisa turned to Lt. Thompson. "I feel better." she said.

"I'm glad you do," Lt Thompson said. Maybe you and Elsa would like to meet us about eight o'clock this evening, and we'll walk down to the Red Cross Club here in Bury St. Edmunds. It's a nice place, and you'll like the director, Tom Anderson. Everyone likes him."

"That sounds good to me."

Elsa, who was listening, chimed in, "Me, too?"

"Of course, and Larry, too." Lt. Thompson said. "We couldn't do without you."

"Do what without us?" Larry cracked."From here on you girls can call us by our first names. I'm Larry and he's Andy."

"That's much better, Larry." Elsa agreed.

"See you in about an hour in the lobby," Lt Thompson said as he and Lt. Aronson turned to leave.

When the officers had gone, Lisa turned to Elsa with a question that had been bothering her. "You know that Harold Cross. He didn't open his mouth all evening. Why do you suppose he was so silent?"

"I haven't the foggiest"' Elsa answered. "And what's more, I don't care if he never opens his mouth around me again. He's some kind of weirdo."

"Maybe," Lisa said."Maybe that's what he is, but I'm not sure."

When the girls came down the stairs that evening, Larry and Andy stood to greet them, and for the first time, Lisa noticed that both of them were exceptionally handsome men. It crossed her mind that almost all of the men in the army and air forces were good-looking men...the world's finest. And Andy, with his tall, muscular build, wavy dark hair, blue eyes and dimples, wearing the air force leather flying jacket with silver wings on his chest, probably was one of the best looking men she'd ever seen. She thought he looked like Clark Gable...only better. Lisa was happy and excited when she took Andy's arm as they started down the steps from the porch of the Angel Hotel to the cobblestone street below. It promised to be a good evening, and it was.

It was a dark wintry night, too dark to see the street curbs, but Andy confidently led the way past the ancient Abbey and down narrow streets bordered with row houses.

"It's spooky, isn't it?" Lisa said.

Andy was reassuring: "No, it's O.K. I've been this way several times already."

When they reached the Red Cross club, the director, Tom Anderson came to the door to greet them. He was a ruddy, pleasant-looking man, who was extremely proud of the club he had established for G.I.'S in Bury St. Edmunds. Mr. Anderson showed his guests through the restaurant and a games room with card tables and a ping-pong table. Then he invited them to his own quarters upstairs where there were several comfortable chairs, a divan, a desk, a coffee table and a stand lamp. These things might seem quite ordinary, and not worthy of mention, but as Lisa and Elsa were to learn, they were impossible to obtain in war-time England.

A group of about eight GI's were lined up at Mr. Anderson's desk waiting for him to work out various problems they had encountered. The process took over an hour. In the meantime, Lisa and Elsa and the officers were greeted by Mr. Anderson's two Red Cross assistants, Elizabeth Parker and Gertrude Smith. And shortly the group was joined by three clubmobile girls who were stationed in the area.

It was an interesting and revealing evening for Elsa and Lisa because it was their first contact with Red Cross workers in the field. Mr. Anderson and the five American girls stationed there were already doing a job!

Mr. Anderson was responsible for the initial establishment of the club in Bury St. Edmunds. It was he who scrounged furniture, obtained rations from the English market, hired an English staff, installed a doughnut making machine, and attended to the finances of the club. Mr. Anderson's assistants, Gertrude and Elizabeth, conducted a recreation program for the soldiers on leave, established a list of English dancing partners who were screened for respectability, hired a hall and music for dances, organized picnics, hikes, and other social functions.

The clubmobile girls Esther and Ann, had an entirely different job, and a different function to perform. Affectionatly called "Doughnut Dollies" by the GI's they served, the clubmobile girls manned a converted bus which had a serving counter cut into one side, and was equipped with large coffee urns and a doughnut-making machine. Each morning the clubmobile girls and their English driver drove to an American airfield where they parked their bus near the flight line where they cooked and served thousands of doughnuts, and prepared tens of thousands of cups of coffee for the airmen who crowded about their bus. Beside the "snack" the girls played popular American music from a loudspeaker that had been hooked up to a record player. The clubmobile girls and their doughnut-making bus were especially popular with the American men because they were a reminder of home.

The Red Cross girls and Mr. Anderson were shocked when Lisa told them about their first night in a disreputable hotel.

"You could have stayed here with us," Mr. Anderson said. "We have a room we keep especially for guests. After this, you are to consider me as you would a father. I will be here to help you however I can."

"Now you tell us." Elsa said.

"I'm grateful." Lisa added. "It's nice to know we have someone to turn to because I really don't think it's going to be easy."

"No," Mr. Anderson said. "It will be very hard."

Reluctantly they left the Red Cross club early, because it was the custom of the Angel Hotel to lock the outside door at ten o'clock in the evening. Tenants coming in later were required to ring the doorbell, causing inconvenience to the manageress who would get out of bed to come down and open the door.

Walking back to the Angel Hotel, Lisa was surprised that everyone in the little village seemed to be asleep. If any life stirred behind the blacked-out windows, she could neither see nor hear it. All four of them strained their eyes trying to see their way in the darkness, and as they groped along the cobble-stoned street, their footsteps echoed and re-echoed and sounded so loud that Lisa found herself tip-toeing, so that the people in the shadowy houses would not hear.

Suddenly Andy stopped. "Look ahead," he said as he took Lisa's hand in his own.

Lisa peered into the darkness ahead and saw the outline of Elsa and Larry in an embrace. "Well," she said, "that's the first time I've seen Elsa fall for a man."

Andy pulled Lisa toward him. "How about you?" he asked softly.

Lisa's heart missed a beat. Confusion overwhelmed her, and she closed her eyes in an effort to gather her thoughts. Andy pulled her closer, lifted her chin, and kissed her firmly on the lips. Lisa found herself kissing him back with a passion she had not known for a long time. Lisa was kissing Andy, but she was thinking of Steve.

CHAPTER 9

A JOB TO DO

Mickey was at the Angel Hotel at nine o'clock A.M. on the dot as he said he would be. Lisa and Elsa were ready. A trip to the station, confirmed that their luggage had not arrived, and they set out for the air base in a military command car. The GI driver took them through the cobble-stoned streets of the village and out on to the King's Highway which led through the lovely countryside of rural England. It was a picture-postcard landscape of orange, bronze, and green; neatly cultivated plots of land, cross-stitched with hedgerows, like an old-fashioned crazy quilt. Shortly they came to a cluster of trees, and on the left, got their first glimpse of the runways where several B-26 medium bombers, the first of their kind in England, squatted there like great, overgrown bumble bees. Off to the right was the living area where American G.I.'S were walking along the roadways and swarming into low-slung elongated huts that were camouflaged with a mosaic blending of brown, yellow and tan. These were the British Nissen huts, which resembled American Quonset huts, except that the walls on each end were brick.

The command car turned down a tree-shaded lane, past a score of Nissen huts, and finally came to a stop in a small courtyard that divided a small hut from a group of five interconnected large ones.

"This is it." Mickey announced.

Lisa thought it wasn't anything like the cozy night spot she had imagined it would be. The small hut, she learned, was to become her living quarters, and the five large ones were to be made into a recreational club. Mickey led the way into the club through a long dark hallway with small storage rooms on either side. At the end, there was a tremendous kitchen, furnished with three immense coal ranges, forming three sides of a square in the center of the room. The fourth side was formed by a ceiling-high contraption that looked like nothing Lisa had ever seen before, but which she later learned was a fish and chips fryer which she soon converted into a donut maker.

Along the walls of the kitchen were long worktables and three dishwashing tubs that looked like laundry tubs. It wasn't exactly a bride's idea of a dream-kitchen, and adding to its naturally dismal aspect was a man-made chaos that Mickey explained with a chuckle: "The English NAAFI was running a club here until last week," he said. "They were sore at being run out to make way for the Red Cross, so they piled the stoves full of bricks and junk, and tore all of the linoleum off the floors and serving counters."

"That was a terrible thing for them to do," Lisa said.

"Bitches! They hate us." Elsa remarked.

"This is carrying hate too far," Lisa replied.

Lisa was sure that Mickey had made a mistake throwing anybody out to make way for her, because she was quite certain that this was a job with which she could not cope.

There was a serving room just off the kitchen with two long counters, one on each side of the room, opening into separate dining halls. British army protocol separated enlisted men from non-commissioned officers for meals. Lisa knew that she would have to change that immediately.

A small office opened off the serving room, where Lisa would spend many uncomfortable hours struggling over account books that wouldn't come out right, and conferring with employees who wouldn't do right.

There was one huge building which was to become the snack bar. Here and there about the room, as was the case in the other buildings as well, were several pot-bellied coal stoves.

All of the floors were bare cement, and the metal rounded walls were painted a bilious army tan. There was no furniture in any of the five buildings, but the windows throughout were equipped with black curtains on double runners, to comply with black-out regulations.

When Lisa had finished her tour of the buildings she sat down on a serving counter. "I'm lonely already."she said.

"With three thousand men around, you'll be lucky to be alone for even one night," Elsa cracked.

Turning to Mickey, Elsa asked. "Is my club as bad as this one?"

"Worse," Mickey answered matter-of-factly, "but it's smaller."

"Well this one could be cut in half and it would still be too big for an air force of giants," Elsa remarked.

Lisa remained silent, thinking that the whole project was hopeless.

"Now," Mickey said cheerfully, "I'll take you to meet the Special Service Officer. He has charge of things around here, and he's a hard man to get along with. Yes. He is sure a hard man!"

"All I need right now" Lisa said, "is a hard man to deal with."

Mickey's opinion of the Special Service Officer did nothing to make Lisa feel better about her situation, particularly when she recalled that someone had said something about getting along with the Special Service officer at all costs, underlined!

The Special Service Officer, Lt. Fred Winston, was sitting at a desk answering three telephones at once when they entered his office. He barked instructions first into one phone and then into another, and generally appeared to be the busiest man Lisa had ever seen. He was also a fine looking man...a man's man that women would admire too. His smile of greeting was pleasant, and there was a twinkle in his eyes that were as blue as the summer skies over his native Oklahoma. Lisa thought he wasn't anything like the hard man Mickey had described, and she had a feeling that she would get along with Lt. Winston much better than Mickey had.

When Lt. Winston rose to acknowledge Mickey's introductions, Lisa noted that he was very tall, several inches over six feet. He shook hands all around, and immediately became business-like again. "Have you seen the club?" he asked.

"Yes," Mickey replied. "Yes, we sure have. Now I've got to take Elsa to her club. Would you look after Lisa for me until I get back?"

Lt. Winston said he would. But he frowned, and didn't seem too happy about it. Lisa wanted to say that she really didn't need a baby-sitter, but she remembered that someone had said that she had to get along with the Special Service Officer at all costs.

Lt. Winston offered Lisa a chair and she sat down and waited and waited while Lt. Winston worked at his job of directing the war to ultimate victory for the Allied cause. Lt. Winston was so engrossed in his work that Lisa was sure he had forgotten that she was there.

From telephone conversations, and bits of information gleaned from various visitors to his desk, Lisa learned that besides being Special Service Officer, Lt. Winston was also mess officer, commanding officer of the headquarters detachment of which Lisa was the newest member, club officer in charge of social activities and entertainment for all post officers, liquor procurement officer and censor. The last gave Lisa cause for concern. Lt. Winston might own her body and soul, which apparently he did, but she thought that reading her letters was carrying his prerogatives too far. Nevertheless, from then on, Lt. Winston read every letter Lisa wrote and every one she received, and often he blocked out whole paragraphs which Lisa was sure had nothing to do with security. It was extremely disconcerting.

Soon Lisa began having second thoughts about how well she was going to get along with Lt. Winston. She was sure that he was one of those super-efficient people who never in the world could understand or perhaps even tolerate the likes of people who enjoyed mixing business with pleasure now and then.

As doubts entered Lisa's mind, Lt. Winston proceeded with his work until at last he was finished, or at least had completed those tasks which he regarded as more important than talking to a bewildered Red Cross worker. Then he turned to Lisa to ask a question she could not answer.

"When," he asked, "do you expect to open the club?"

Lt. Winston might just as well have asked Lisa when she expected to fly to the moon. But Lisa realized that a direct question from a superior officer required at least a reply of some kind, so she countered. "When do you think it should open?"

"Not later than the end of next week," he answered, just as if he were saying something rational.

Lisa didn't say anything. One does not, she thought, tell a brand new boss that one doesn't have the slightest idea where to begin the job to which one has been assigned. She waited for a lead.

"I think we might go over to the club and look things over," he suggested.

Lisa agreed readily, mentally patting herself on the back for getting out of a tight spot.

Back at the club a strange thing happened. It may have been that the sun which had been in hiding for several days, was now casting rosy hues over the soot-grimed walls and cement floors, for suddenly the job didn't seem so hopeless. Lisa burst forth into enthusiastic planning. She spoke of what one could do with an enclosed stadium like this if you could paint the Snack Bar walls a pale decorator-blue, and drape the windows with gay cretonne curtains.

"Then," she said, "I'll paint the lounge room a soft beige with pale blue drapes, and put overstuffed chairs and sofas around it. The games room will be a gay and giddy yellow, with ping-pong tables and dart boards. The library will be green with thousands of books and, the card room will be rose-colored. Perhaps, if I've time, I will even plant flowers along the borders of the sidewalks, and put flower boxes at the windows... "

Lisa stopped for breath, and noted that Lt. Winston was staring at her in amazement. "How," he asked, "will you accomplish all this by next week-end?"

Lisa realized that she sounded just like Mickey when she said, "Yes. Next week-end. I had forgotten that."

Lt. Winston appeared not to have noticed, and like a parent explaining to a backward child, he tried to tell Lisa why it was important that the club should open at once. "You see," he explained, "the NAAFI was here until last week, and when I agreed to ask them to leave, I was given a definite assurance by the representative of the American Red Cross that this club would be open again within a week. The men will be expecting it to open, and will not be tolerant of a delay. I didn't expect much to be done while Mickey was here alone, because, well...because he's not the kind of person to get things done. But now that you're here, I'll expect the club to open on schedule."

Lisa felt sick. "You expect me to open a club by the end of next week," she said, "and I haven't any equipment, or any money, or any supplies, or any help. I don't think I'm going to get it open ever."

Lt. Winston frowned. "Are you telling me that you haven't had any instructions about opening this club next week end?"

Lisa noticed that Lt. Winston's face had turned pale, a warning, as she learned later, that he was becoming angry. "A fine thing!" he exploded. "Just fine! I kick out the NAAFI, and the Red Cross sends a girl down here to open the club, and nothing to open it with."

Lisa was overwhelmed with the hopelessness of it all. Opening her pocketbook, she took out the stop watch that Mr. Allen had given her, and handed it to Lt. Winston. "You may have this," she said. "It's all the equipment I have. Mr. Allen, who is in charge of the field staff, gave it to me, and told me to keep it because it is very hard to obtain. But I won't need it because I can't do this job. I'm going back to London and transfer to some other department. I can't face all these soldiers day after day expecting me to do something about opening the club, and not being able to do it. If I had some help, I might try, but Mickey is all there is, and I'm not sure he's any help at all."

Lt. Winston put the stop watch back in Lisa's hand, and looked at her without sympathy. "My heart bleeds for you," he said. "If there's a time when you want some help, come around." Then he turned about and left.

Lisa wandered dismally into the kitchen where she perched on one of the work tables because there were no chairs. She was alone, and it was quiet there, and she could think. She thought about the commitment she had made when she joined the Red Cross. She thought about the men on the base she had pledged to serve, who soon would be flying B-26 bombers over enemy territory. She thought about Lt. Hanson and his men, who had already seen action in the South Pacific, and were now on a submarine somewhere in the Atlantic Ocean. And she thought about Steve. Lisa felt ashamed that she had threatened to give up on her first assignment because she had run into difficulties. She understood what Lt. Winston meant when he said, "My heart bleeds for you,"and she made up her mind to apologize to Lt. Winston and to tell him that she would see it through, whatever the problems.

Lisa was still sitting on the table when Mickey and Elsa came back from her station. Elsa didn't look happy.

"What's yours like?" Lisa asked.

"It's worse than this one," Elsa answered dismally. "More mud outside and smaller stoves inside. Even my quarters are bitchy."

"Ye Gods!"Lisa exclaimed. "I haven't even seen my quarters yet. Let's go out and see what it's like."

Lisa led the way down the hall, out into the little courtyard, past a row of empty garbage cans, and into the door of the little hut. She noticed that once there had been linoleum on the floor of the entrance hall, but the NAAFI predecessors had torn it out leaving tar-stained concrete with broken pieces of linoleum lying about.

There were four bedrooms in the hut, and a bath. Each room was equipped with a coal stove and black-out curtains, but there was no other furniture. However, Lisa received an unexpected and pleasant surprise. An R.A.F. soldier was painting the walls of one of the bedrooms a pale blue. He was standing on a ladder, and grinned at Lisa from his perch. "The gov'ner said there'd be a Yank girl living here, so I'm brightening the place up a bit."

"Who's the Gov'ner?" Lisa asked.

"Leftenant Winston," he replied.

At that moment Lisa was surprised again. The door to the hut opened, and several GI's came in carrying furniture. There was an iron bed, a walnut chest of drawers, and a cardboard wardrobe. The airmen placed the furniture about the room, and with the freshly painted walls, the effect was really not bad, almost cozy, and Lisa was pleased.

The RAF painter had finished his job, and he climbed down from his ladder, picked up his paint cans and brushes and smiled at Lisa. "Jolly nice, isn't it?" he said.

"Indeed it is," Lisa agreed, and turning to Mickey she said, "Do I have you to thank for the furniture?"

"No," Mickey answered, "Lt. Winston ordered it."

For the first time, Elsa spoke up. "Do you suppose I could stay with you tonight, Lisa? I need some time."

"Of course," Lisa said. "We'll get another bed, and we'll have to get some blankets and sheets, and I'm sure we can get some for you, too."

Mickey demurred. "I'm not sure you can do that without Lt. Winston's approval. He's in charge around here."

Lisa didn't want to tell Mickey that Lt. Winston was displeased with her, and she turned again to the RAF painter. "Do you know where I can get the equipment we need?" she asked.

"Right-o, Miss,"he said as he led the way outside. "Come, I'll show you."

He pointed down the road. "Straight ahead, third building on your left; you cawn't miss it."

"Thank you," Lisa said, and she and Elsa started off down the road, attracting attention as they went. There were soldiers everywhere, and it seemed that they were all looking at Lisa and Elsa. It was like a child's poem that Lisa remembered:

"Wolves here; wolves there.
Big wolves, and little wolves, everywhere!
Hundreds of wolves;
Thousands of wolves;
Millions and billions and trillions of wolves."

Self-consciously, Lisa and Elsa said "Hello" to those they met on the walk and waved to those who watched from doorways and windows. They turned into the walk leading to the third hut and entered the door where a tough looking sergeant was seated at a desk. "Is this the quartermaster department?" Lisa asked.

"What can I do for you?" the sergeant asked politely.

Lisa explained her mission and asked for a bed and blankets for Elsa. The sergeant was more than accommodating, and immediately disappeared into a back room. Presently he returned with his arms full of blankets, sheets, and pillows, and was followed by a GI carrying an army bed.

The girls and the airmen walked out of the building into a glaring light of attention. Everyone who saw them reacted. Some gaped; others looked surprised, some laughed, and some made bold remarks. "Say now, Ed,"one soldier called to the sergeant. "How do you do it so soon?"

Back at the quarters, they found that Lt. Winston had joined Mickey and the two of them were impatiently waiting for Lisa and Elsa to return.

"I'm sorry, Lieutenant," Lisa said. "I hope we haven't kept you waiting. Elsa wants to stay here tonight because her quarters aren't quite ready yet. And I want to thank you for getting this one ready for me."

"Oh it was nothing" Lt. Winston said with a smile. "And Elsa is more than welcome. When the sergeant finishes helping you with the beds, I thought you might want to walk over to the mess for dinner. They've started serving already."

Lisa and Elsa thanked Lt. Winston again and said they would hurry.

Sergeant Ed was helpful. Quickly he set up the bed and taught Lisa and Elsa how to make a bunk, army style. Expertly, he mitred the sheets until they were so tight and smooth that he bragged he could bounce a penny on them. Then he repeated the process on each of the eight army blankets he put on top.

"An army cot must be made just so," he smirked, "or you'll find it mighty cold, and that would be too bad."

When the sergeant left, Lt. Winston led the way to the officers' mess hall. Lisa did not know what to expect, but she wasn't prepared for the reality of dining with five hundred officers in the U. S. air force. As they made their way through the chow line, Lisa felt uncomfortably conspicuous. Elsa, however, was smiling and exhilarated. Five hundred handsome young officers in one place with only two girls was some kind of Seventh Heaven for her. As they entered the dining hall and found four seats at one of the long tables that filled the room, Lisa saw Andy at a table with a group of fliers. He nodded and smiled, and when he had finished his meal, he came over to greet her. Larry had also come to the table to see Elsa, and Harold Cross soon came by to welcome them. Lt. Winston was surprised. "Have all of you met before?" he asked.

"Oh yes." Andy said. "We're old friends."

Lt. Winston frowned, and Lisa wondered if he was displeased.

"We met at the Angel Hotel yesterday," she explained hurriedly, "and I met Mr. Cross in London."

Larry, who never bothered to beat about the bush, said, "How about you girls meeting us after you've finished dinner? We'll get a car and drive into town to see if your luggage has come yet. We have to be back early, though, because we're starting training maneuvers early tomorrow morning."

"That's a wonderful idea." Elsa said. "We'll meet you at the club in half an hour."

"Right-o" Andy agreed. "We'll be there. Then he and Larry and Harold Cross left.

Lt Winston made no comment through the dinner, and when he finished, he stood and spoke to Lisa. "We'll get started right after breakfast tomorrow morning. Report to my office."

"Yes Sir," Lisa said, and she wondered if she was supposed to salute.

And as if it were an after-thought, Lt. Winston said: "I think you should know that for your protection, your quarters have been declared off limits to all military personnel on the base."

Lisa said, "Yes Sir."

Larry and Andy were at the club with a command car and driver as they said they would be. They helped the girls into the car, and set off for Bury St. Edmunds. When they arrived at the railroad station luggage department, Lisa and Elsa were delighted to find that their luggage had indeed arrived.

"You see," Lisa said, "They don't hate us after all."

Larry and Andy picked up the luggage and put it in the car, and Andy suggested they go to the Angel Hotel for a gin and bitters before returning to the base. "We'll celebrate our first meeting there," he said.

When they entered the dining room at the Angel Hotel, Andy, showing a sentimental side, asked for the same table where they had met. During a pleasant hour discussing their pasts, Lisa learned that Andy was a graduate of the University of Washington in Seattle, and planned to become a lawyer after his tour of duty in the air force. Larry, who was a college graduate from the University of Oklahoma, had more ambitious plans. After the war he planned to open a business and become a multi-millionaire entrepreneur.

Larry was not surprised when Elsa said she was a dance instructoress. "I could have guessed," he remarked. "You would be a great asset in any business. We'd make a good team."

When Lisa said she had been a newspaper reporter, Andy was surprised. "You don't seem sophisticated enough to be a newspaper woman," he said.

"I'm not sophisticated enough to be an aero club director, either. There's so much I have to learn."

Andy took her hand in his. "Don't worry, you'll do all right, whatever you do."

"This party is getting mushy," Larry said. "We have to return to the base. I thought we might have a little time, but they want us back by nine."

Lisa and Elsa were disappointed. "The evening is just beginning," Elsa complained.

"There's a war going on,"Andy said. "We keep forgetting. I'm sorry, too."

It was a dark and drizzly night as were most nights in East Anglia. Back at the club Larry and Andy lifted the girls' luggage from the car and placed it in Lisa's room. Then Larry said. "Sorry girls, we can't stay longer, we're due back at our quarters in two minutes."

"That's O.K." Lisa said. "You can't stay here, anyway. Lt. Winston said my quarters have been declared off limits to the likes of you and Andy."

Andy grinned. "Lt. Winston has ulterior motives. Has he declared himself off limits as well?"

As Larry and Andy were leaving, the M.P. car that patrolled the area drove by and flashed a search light over the hut.

"We'll probably be court- marshaled for this," Larry said as he put his arms around Elsa for a goodnight kiss.

At the same time, Andy took Lisa into his arms and kissed her gently on the lips. "I'll see you tomorrow night," he said.

CHAPTER 10

THERE'S A WAR GOING ON

It was a dark, mid-winter morning when Lisa and Elsa entered the officers' mess with Mickey. Right after breakfast, Mickey would be driving Elsa to her base some fifteen miles away. "Elsa, it was good to have you here last night," Lisa said as they stood in the chow line.

"It was good for me, too," Elsa answered. "We'll be seeing each other soon. Larry has promised to bring me down whenever he can."

"I'm sure he will."

Larry and Andy had already finished breakfast, and were not in the dining hall when Lisa and Elsa arrived. Lisa remembered that Andy had told her they would begin training maneuvers this day. But she was sorry she didn't see him, and Elsa was sad, too. "I wish I could have said good-bye to Larry," she said.

Mickey and Elsa left right after breakfast, and Lisa reported to Lt. Winston at his office. Lt. Winston offered her a chair, and introduced her to his two sergeants who were instructed to help her in her efforts to open a recreation club for GI's by next week-end.

"You can depend on us," Sergeant Brown said.

"We're very dependable," Sergeant Alexander added.

Lisa smiled. "It's good to know that I am to have help from Lt. Winston and his sergeants. Heaven knows I need help."

Lt. Winston informed Lisa that he had also obtained a detail of GIs to clean up the club. "They will be working today," he said, "and I have a car and driver to take you into town to make arrangements for snack supplies from the Ministry of Food. Sometimes it takes several days for the Ministry to process a request of this magnitude. So be patient, and as nice as possible. I'll meet you at the club in fifteen minutes."

The meeting with the Minister of Food was easier than Lisa had anticipated because Lt. Winston took over. With incredible ease Lt. Winston requested and received promises of food rations for snack items for three thousand men. The minister agreed to have the request processed, and Lt. Winston and Lisa left the premises. Lisa suggested that they might stop for a cup of tea at the Angel Hotel, but Lt. Winston took his job seriously, and he expected no less of Lisa. "We still have work to do at the base," he said.

When the command car neared the base, Lisa observed B-26 bombers flying just above the tree-tops. One roared directly over their heads as it headed towards a run-way, causing Lisa to duck. Lt. Winston put his hand on her shoulder. "It's all right," he said. "B-26 bombers fly low because they were designed to fly beneath enemy radar to attack specific targets. You'll get used to them."

But Lisa was sure that she never would become used to their dare-devil flights. "It seems very dangerous to me when they fly so low and so fast."

"It is dangerous," Lt. Winston said. "That's why the B-26 is called B-Dash-Crash."

Lisa felt a chill. She was thinking of Andy and Larry.

When they arrived at the quarters, Lisa was surprised to see a woman's bicycle standing against the hut. "Whose bicycle is that?"she asked.

Lt. Winston smiled smugly, obviously pleased with himself. "It's yours," he said, "and I have one for Elsa, too. They were left here by the WAAF when the RAF vacated the station. I've been waiting for some women to come along who could use them."

For Lisa it was a wonderful gift, especially in England, where a bicycle was the principle means of transportation. "It's been a long time since I've ridden a bicycle," she said, "I wonder if I can still do it."

"Well, you'll get a chance to try as soon as we check to see what the clean-up detail has done."

"Of course. But first, I want to thank you. It was so good of you to think of a bicycle for me."

Lt. Winston turned towards the club as he answered. "I think you will need it, and I'm glad I could be of help."

The GI detail had done a wonderful job clearing out all of the debris the NAAFI had left, scrubbing the floors and counters in the kitchen and sweeping the floors and cleaning the windows in all of the buildings. "It's like a miracle." Lisa exclaimed. "How did they do it so fast?"

"They want the club to open as soon as possible," Lt. Winston answered.

It was at that point that Lisa mentally made a decision that was to assure success for her mission to build a super GI recreational club on a B-26 base in East Anglia. She had come to the conclusion that Lt. Winston was some kind of dedicated efficiency genius who knew everything about everything, and she decided that she would lay her problems, whatever they might be, on his broad shoulders. It was a wise decision.

"I'll try my best not to disappoint you and the men on this base," Lisa said.

"Good," Lt Winston said. "To begin with you'll have to become acquainted with the Clerk of the Works. No kidding, that's his title. He's the English representative of the Ministry of Air in London. He has his office on the field, and is in charge of all buildings. Actually, he's the watchdog of the Ministry to make certain that we don't wreck the buildings or use too much of the strategic materials. If he likes you, and is so inclined, he can authorize all sorts of things, like paint and linoleum, and an extra bit of coal now and then."

"He sounds very important," Lisa agreed. "I am indeed impressed."

"He is important," Lt Winston emphasized, "We need the things he has, or can get for us. Come along, I'll introduce you."

The Clerk of the Works, Mr. Randolph, was ruddy, tubby and a most obliging man. With great alacrity, he agreed to accompany Lisa and the lieutenant to inspect the club with a view to making it more attractive.

At the club, Lisa pointed out all of the things that she thought must be done at once. "I'd like to have the Snack Bar painted light blue," she suggested.

"That would be jolly," Randolph agreed. "I'll see what can be done about it."

"And I'd like to have the lounge room painted beige; the library in green; the games room, yellow, and the card room, rose."

"Right-o!"

"And I'd like to have two big brick fireplaces built in the library and lounge rooms."

"Precisely!"

"Thank you very much," Lisa said delightedly, "You are really very kind."

"Hmmmmmmmm..." Mr. Randolph replied.

When Mr. Randolph left with a pleasant "Cheerio," Lisa was convinced that a miraculous transition would soon take place at the club. Lt. Winston, too, was impressed by her success. "I'm sure you're going to do all right," he said. "I've been trying to get things from Randolph ever since I've been here without much luck, and you get promises like pennies from Heaven!"

But what neither Lisa nor Lt. Winston knew then, was that all she was getting was promises. Mr. Randolph was possessed of an exaggerated gallantry, and he just couldn't bring himself to say "no" to a woman. Lisa supposed that if she had asked him for a slice of the moon, he would have promised to have it there on her doorstep the next day.

In return for his gallantry, Lisa was supposed not to mind that his promises were never fulfilled, nor were they meant to be.

After Lt. Winston had returned to his office, Lisa went back to her quarters and decided to try out the bicycle. To her surprise, she found she had not forgotten how to do it, and she pedalled away down the road with gay abandon, failing to look where she was going, when suddenly she came face to bumper with a small English car known as a Crosley. She turned quickly, and landed in a heap alongside the road. Her collapse was uproariously funny to the soldiers who were always everywhere and saw everything. Embarrassed, she got up, dusted herself off, and discovered that the man driving the Crosley was Mickey, no less. He had stopped the car and was laboriously extricating his huge body from the tiny car in an effort to help her.

Mickey pointed to the Crosley. "It's mine," he said, as pleased as an overgrown child with a new toy, "How do you like it?"

"I think it's wonderful," she said. "Perfectly wonderful!"

Mickey was in a magnanimous mood. "You can drive it anytime you want to," he offered.

Lisa laughed. "And you can ride my bike anytime you want to."

It had been a good day for Lisa, and she was in a good mood when Mickey suggested that they walk over to the officers' mess for dinner. When she walked into the dining hall, however, her spirits fell when she did not see Andy and Larry there. Harold Cross was eating at the table where she and Mickey sat, and soon came over. "May I join you?" he asked.

Lisa nodded, and Harold sat down. Then he turned to Lisa. "I wanted to see you tonight," he said. "I want you to know that I am here, and if ever you need help you can call on me. It will be tough on you from now on. And... don't expect too much of Andy. He has his hands full, too."

Lisa could not quite follow what Harold Cross was saying, but she knew he was indicating that missions over enemy territory would be starting. She was grateful to Harold Cross for understanding the apprehension she would be feeling from now on, but she wondered how he seemed to know everything that was going on.

When Lisa retired to her quarters that evening, she realized that she was quite alone, and she was very cold. She discovered that she had no coal for the stove, and there was no heat, and no warm water. She decided to go to bed immediately, even though it was not yet dark, and she lay awake, shivering for some time before she felt reasonably comfortable. She listened to the sound of army vehicles driving up and down the road, and the subdued voices of soldiers as they walked past her quarters, and she tried to identify strange sounds that she did not recognize. And she was thinking of Andy and Larry and all the rest of the fliers who would soon be in grave danger. It was almost too much to bear, but she knew that she could not let anxiety overwhelm her. She had to keep going.

At last Lisa fell asleep, only to be awakened by the grating sound of the Tanoy loudspeaker system. Soon she heard a man's voice metallically saying: "Blue Alert! Put out all lights, cigarettes and matches. Wait for further orders."

Then there was a pause for several minutes before the voice again grated over the loudspeaker. "Yellow Alert. Prepare for enemy action."

Then another pause, not so long, and the voice rapped out: "Red Alert! Enemy planes are directly overhead. Take cover."

Lisa stared into the darkness of the hut, too frightened to move. "Take cover," the man said. "Now where in the world would I take cover?" she wondered.

Lisa remembered that she had been told that there were air-raid trenches on the field, but she didn't know where they were, and besides, she had been told that customarily several inches of water was standing in them. Lisa didn't want to get bombed in her bed, but neither did she want to get out in freezing weather, climb into an underground shelter, and stand in several inches of icy water with a bunch of GI's.

Lisa pulled the blankets over her head like a frightened child and stayed where she was. Soon she heard the drone of planes high overhead. They came nearer and nearer; then gradually faded away, and she knew that she was not the target that night.

The Tanoy voice came back to life. "The enemy planes have passed. All Clear."

It was the first of many such nights for Lisa. Fortunately, as time went by, she actually became accustomed to the sound of the Tanoy loudspeakers and the drone of enemy planes overhead.

Lisa didn't go back to sleep for a long time that night. She was lonely, homesick, and frightened, and she didn't like being the only woman on a base with three thousand men. Lisa discovered that a girl can't possibly date three thousand men; she can't even talk to three thousand men, and when there are thousands, they become masses instead of individuals, and she found herself alone amongst them. But Lisa soon learned that all three thousand of the American men who lived on the B-26 bomber base in East Anglia, England, would be kind and protective of her, and would try in every way to help her cope with the problems she faced. Lisa would be forever grateful to them...every one.

CHAPTER 11

WAITING FOR THE PLANES

It was a clear morning after the unsettling night when enemy bombers had flown overhead. Lisa walked out of her hut and noticed that the sky was clear of planes, and no soldiers could be seen wandering about. It was quiet and somehow different. She walked into the kitchen, and found a young man busily stoking one of the cooking stoves."Hello," she said. "Are you the detail Lt. Winston said he would send over?"

The young man looked down at his GI shoes and mumbled something that sounded like nothing at all. He was short and dark, and he spoke with a Spanish accent when he spoke at all, which wasn't often. But he looked very good to Lisa. "What's your name?" she asked.

"Private Nick Martinez."

"Well Nick, I'm very glad to see you. I've got lots to do here, and I don't know what to do first. What would you suggest?"

"Coal."

"Yes," Lisa agreed. "But where do we get it?"

"The Clerk of the Jerks," Nick replied.

"You mean the Clerk of the Works. His name is Mr. Randolph. He's a very nice man. I've met him already. Wait right here and I'll be back with some coal."

Lisa climbed on her bike, and pedalled down the road to the office of the Clerk of the Works. Mr. Randolph was as jolly and friendly as ever, but was of little help on the coal situation. "Coal is rationed, y'know," he said. "But I'll give you an official request form. Properly filled in, it will be given consideration, and in a week or so perhaps, you will be in receipt of your allotment."

Crestfallen, Lisa filled out the form; thanked Mr. Randall for nothing at all, and biked back to the club.

Nick listened quietly to her explanation that there would be no coal for a week or so. When she had finished, he outlined a plan that had been in his mind all along. " I will squeeze under the fence around the coal pile; you hold the bag outside, and keep watch for M.P.'s."

"And the Clerk of the Works."

"Him too."

Lisa and Nick slipped out of the club, and walked several blocks to the fence that surrounded the huge coal pile. Nick quickly dug a hole under the fence with a spade until he could squeeze his small body inside. Then he filled the bag Lisa held outside. On the way back to the club, Lisa noted that there were no planes maneuvering that morning.

"No," Nick said. "They're on a mission today."

"I thought so." Lisa said. "I hope they come back safely."

But Lisa was apprehensive. She had not heard from Andy the evening before, and she knew he was probably on the mission. It was her first experience of waiting and dreading...an ordeal she was to endure many times.

Back at the club Nick broke up some packing boxes for kindling, and expertly started a fire in the little firebox beneath the water heater. By then it was time for lunch. Nick locked up, and they left to go to their separate mess halls.

Lisa returned first and immediately saw that something had gone very wrong. Boiling water was gushing into the air above the kitchen, bubbling and steaming over the roof.

"Ye Gods!" she exclaimed out loud. "The thing has exploded."

She stared in consternation for a moment, then ran and climbed on her bike and set out for the Clerk of the Works.

She burst into Mr. Randolph's office, and he looked up with a startled expression on his face because she was screaming at him: "Come quick, The hot water tank has exploded, and it's boiling over the roof."

Mr. Randolph's face relaxed. "It's supposed to do that," he said calmly. "When the water gets too hot, it goes over the roof to keep the tank from exploding."

"When will it stop?" she asked.

"When the hot water has flowed out."

"Will we have to heat more then?"

"Precisely."

"Oh," Lisa said, greatly relieved. She was thinking the British really were ingenious, and she started out the door.

Mr. Randolph stopped her with a question."Would you mind telling me where you got the coal?"

"I borrowed it," Lisa replied, thinking it wasn't any worse to tell a lie than to steal, and now she had done both.

"Hmmmmmmm," Mr. Randolph said.

When she returned to the club, Lisa found Nick sitting on a garbage can in the courtyard surveying the hot water bubbling across the roof.

"I think I quit this job," he said. "I think I go back to the garbage detail."

"Oh no, you can't do that Nick," Lisa exclaimed."I need you. I can't do without you. Besides, Mr. Randolph says it's supposed to do that to keep from exploding."

Nick turned his big brown eyes towards Lisa as comprehension dawned slowly, and she knew he'd stay when he got up and unlocked the kitchen door. Inside, everything was as they had left it. There was no sign that anything had gone wrong.

Nick busily set about setting a fire in the big stove, and Lisa picked up a cloth and started scrubbing the counters. Suddenly, they were interrupted in their work by the sound of planes. The planes had returned from the mission, and were circling to land. Lisa and Nick ran outside to watch.

Presently Nick said: "They've all come back."

"How do you know?" Lisa inquired.

"I counted," Nick said simply.

Joy overcame Lisa, and she began to cry.

"Why are you crying ?" Nick asked. "They've all come back."

"I know. It's just that...just that I'm so relieved."

Nick shook his head as he and Lisa turned towards the club to finish their work.

Lisa was interrupted by Mickey who came into the kitchen looking glum. He had a rule book in his hand and a large fore-finger pressed firmly on a specific item therein.

Lisa laid down the cloth with which she had been cleaning a window above the dishwashing tubs, and wiped her hands on a grimy piece of muslin that she had tied around her waist before she touched Mickey's precious book. She took it from him and read:

"The field director, alone, will contact the military on all matters relating to Red Cross activities on all American air fields in the European Theater of Operations."

After she had read the directive, Lisa turned to Mickey. He was uncomfortably shuffling his foot back and forth in a semi-circle on the floor.

"You shouldn't have asked Lt. Winston for a detail," he said."You see, it says so right here."

"Yes I read it. I shouldn't have done it, but..."

"It's all right this time," Mickey interrupted, apparently relieved that Lisa had confessed her guilt. "I just wanted you to know, just wanted you to know, that's all."

"All right," Lisa said. "I have a lot of questions. Please sit down so we can talk."

Mickey sat down on the counter. "O.K." he said, "Fire away."

"First," what are the financial procedures I am supposed to follow? I will need money to buy food, pay for help, and to use as change when I open the club."

Mickey replied that he had no money for those purposes, and he didn't know where, when, or if he could get any. So that matter was settled.

In answer to Lisa's questions about furniture and cooking utensils, Mickey was a little more encouraging, but no more helpful. "There will be some here shortly," he said mysteriously. "Wait and see, you'll have everything you need before long."

"But when?" Lisa persisted.

"I'm not sure," Mickey answered, rubbing his jaw thoughtfully, "but you'll have some. I'm sure of that."

After Mickey left, Lisa didn't feel like working any longer. She sat on the edge of the work table and watched Nick busily blackening the stove tops. He worked quickly and efficiently, completely absorbed in what he was doing; his face serene. It must be nice, she thought, to have just one job to do, and only one master to serve. It must be nice not to be worrying about carrying out directives from Red Cross headquarters, even when they conflicted with the army's idea of what should be done, or of carrying out the army's demands even when they contradicted orders from the Red Cross. To say nothing about trying to get along with the British Clerk of the Works. It would be wonderful to know you were doing your job well, and not be bothered that you might be letting down the Red Cross, the G.I.'S and the people back home who put up the money. It would be wonderful just to do what someone else told you to do, and not have to make decisions for yourself or be responsible for them after they were made.

Lisa knew that she had to talk to Lt. Winston. She donned her coat and cap, informed Nick that she would be back soon, and left for Lt. Winston's office.

Sergeant Alexander, Lt. Winston's right hand man, was a curly haired lothario who ram-rodded the various projects proposed by the Special Service Office; who procured liquid refreshments from London for the bar in the officers' club, who ran the projector for the movies on the field, and who found time to court a fabulous number of girls from Bury St. Edmunds. Sergeant Alexander and Lt. Winston were in conference when Lisa arrived. She sat down to wait, but this time the wait was short.

"Well, we've got company," Lt. Winston greeted her. "Sergeant, you can wait until I've finished with the Red Cross, can't you?"

"Yes Sir!" Sergeant Alexander answered, exaggerating his Texas drawl to emphasize his willingness. "I can always wait for the Red Cross!"

"How are things going?" the Lieutenant asked.

"They aren't going at all; they're just standing still," Lisa replied. "In fact, that's what I came to see you about."

"Go ahead."

"Well, I asked Mickey if I would have some chairs, tables and equipment soon. He said I would, but he wouldn't say when, or where it would come from, or how much there would be. Do you know anything about it?"

"No, and I doubt if Mickey does, either," Lt. Winston answered thoughtfully. "In any case, you can't wait until he lets you in on the secret. I can get some tables and chairs for you from the quartermaster. I've loaned a radio-phonograph and some records to the town club, and I can get them back, because they've got a new one from Red Cross headquarters. I can lend you some dishes and coffee makers from the mess hall. You'll have to buy food on the open market, because the Red Cross is not entitled to quartermaster rations. But you have taken care of that through the Ministry of Food, and so you're all right there. You'll have to talk to Mickey about payment for food supplies. If he calls the Red Cross headquarters, I'm sure they'll help. If not, I'll talk to Mr. Anderson at the town club. The important thing is to get this club open. We can make improvements later.

"Yes, Sir," Lisa said with emphasis. She was relieved, and grateful that Lt. Winston was there. He was a genius, indeed.

When Lisa left Lt. Winston's office she was in a high mood again, and when she reached the club, she was delighted to see Andy standing on the walk, holding a bicycle, smiling and waiting for her. "I thought you might like to go for a bike ride down a romantic country lane," he said.

"I'd love it," Lisa said. "Wait just a minute and I'll be with you."

Lisa ran through the club and out the back door to her hut where her bicycle was standing against the wall. In just a minute she was back on the front walk with Andy as she promised, and they mounted their bikes and rode off. It was their first time together without other people about. When they stopped at an opening in the hedgerow overlooking a green meadow, Andy dismounted and Lisa followed suit. Andy took Lisa in his arms and said."Do you know that this is the first time we've been alone?'

"Yes," Lisa said, "but I'm not frightened."

"I hope not, because there will be many more times for us, and I don't want you to be frightened. I just want you to be happy."

Andy took Lisa in his arms and kissed her. It was a long passionate kiss that said more than words could ever say. Lisa knew that there truly would be many more times.

Lisa and Andy were starting to mount their bikes again when they saw a woman slowly walking along the path towards them. She was a nice looking woman, probably in early middle age. When she was within hearing distance, Andy spoke to her. "Good evening, Ma'am," he said.

"Good evening young man," she said. "You are an American?"

"Yes, and this young lady is also an American with the American Red Cross."

"It's a pleasure, I'm sure. I live up the path a way. Would you like a cup of tea?"

"That would be lovely," Lisa said.

"Lead the way. We'll follow," Andy added. "My name is Andy Thompson and this is Lisa Medina."

The lady smiled. "I'm Amy Major," she said, "My husband is Fred Major. He will enjoy visiting with you."

Amy led them to a thatched cottage alongside the lane. Inside a coal fire was keeping the cottage warm, and a tea pot was already on the table, covered with a"cozy," the unique method English people have of keeping tea hot during a long tea-time.

Fred Major rose to greet them with a friendly smile. He was a good-looking man, slightly bent, but still agile. "Just in time for tea," he said, while hurrying to lay two more cups on the table.

They were making small talk as new acquaintances do, and enjoying the extraordinarily good tea that English people always brew, when Lisa noticed a photograph of a handsome young man in the uniform of the R.A.F. on the fireplace mantel.

"Is that a photograph of your son?' she asked.

Amy's smile faded, and her face turned sad. "Yes," she said. "He was killed last year with the R.A.F."

"I'm so sorry," Lisa said quickly. "We keep forgetting that the British people have been at war a long time."

"We're just beginning," Andy added. "And we're just beginning to understand how bad it is. I'm very sorry."

"You don't know how much your visit has meant to us," Amy said. "I hope you'll come back."

"It's a date," Andy said with a smile. We'll be back as soon as we can."

Amy and Fred both smiled. "Wonderful," Amy said.

Lisa and Andy kept their promise, and in the days to come they often stopped on their bike trips to visit with Amy and Fred and to share tea and biscuits with them. Sometimes Lisa and Andy added their own treats of candy and canned Spam and a special treat of fresh doughnuts.

Lisa and Andy were quiet and subdued as they biked back to the base. There were no more illusions for them. Both knew the perils that lay ahead. It was the beginning for them of a different kind of life. Lisa would be busy establishing a recreation club on the base. Andy would be preparing for increasing numbers of missions over enemy territory. Lisa would be agonizing over the dangers he would be facing, praying for his safe return, and cherishing the days and nights when he would be free.

When Lisa and Andy arrived at the club, they parked their bikes along the wall of Lisa's hut. Then Andy took Lisa in his arms and held her in a tight embrace. "I'd like to come in, Lisa," he said. "But I don't want to cause trouble for you, or for me. We're not playing games now, and however much I want to hold you in my arms and make love, it will have to wait for another time and another place."

"I know," Lisa whispered. "I'll be waiting for you Andy, hoping and praying, and doing my job the best I can."

"One other thing," Andy said. "I can't be of much help to you. We will be doing missions from now on, and there will be briefings and tough missions and de-briefings, and at times I will be exhausted. I think you should depend as much as you can on Lt. Winston. He's a dedicated and efficient man, and I'll try not to be jealous."

"You have no cause to be jealous. I agree that Lt. Winston is some kind of efficiency genius, but he has no interest in me, so put that out of your mind."

"I'm not sure about that, but I'll try not to think about it. As soon as I can get some free time, I want to talk to you about you and me and some things I've been thinking about."

"I'll be waiting."

Andy touched his cap in a quick salute, mounted his bike and left, and once again Lisa was alone. She sat down on the cot and tuned into the radio on the night stand. Vera Lynn, the British radio sensation was singing a famous war-time song:

"I'll Pray for You.
While You're Away
Each Night and Day
I'll Pray for You."

+++

I'll Pray for You
Til Troubles Cease
And You and I
Will Live in Peace."

Lisa bowed her head and prayed: "Please, God, lay Your Hand on his shoulder, and keep him safe."

CHAPTER 12

THE BRITISH MINISTRIES AND OTHER TRIBULATIONS

The British Ministries were new and strange phenomena for Lisa at first, but she soon learned that it was impossible to get along as a Red Cross club director in England, unless one had at least a nodding acquaintance with the Ministries of Air, Labour, Works, Supply, Food, and Health.

In the midst of chaos and confusion, lines of authority were beginning to become clear to Lisa. She was always and forever under the jurisdiction of the American Red Cross headquarters in London, whose directives were delivered to her by Mickey whenever he thought it advisable.

On the field, Lisa was under the jurisdiction of the Commanding Officer, whose orders came through the Special Service Officer, Lt. Winston.

Lisa was to carry on operations in buildings belonging to the Air Ministry, under the supervision of Mr. Randolph. For food, she was dependent upon the Ministry of Food; for furniture and equipment, upon the Ministry of Works and the Ministry of Supply; for help, upon the Ministry of Labour. If her employees should become ill, they were immediately taken under the healing wing of the Ministry of Health.

Lisa sometimes felt that it would take someone with the brain of an Einstein and the dexterity of a Houdini to walk a peaceful path between all of them.

Even a simple decision on when to open the club became a cause for controversy. Mickey said that the Red Cross didn't expect to open for at least a month; certainly not until a manageress and an accountant arrived from headquarters. "You just can't do it," he said, pulling the rule book from his pocket. "It says right here that each club has to have an accountant and a manageress before it can be opened...See?"

"Yes, I see," Lisa answered. "But when are they coming? Lt. Winston says the club will have to open at the end of the week. He has already assured the

Colonel that it will open then, and the G.I.'S expect it. I can't poke my nose out the door without a dozen or more men asking me when the club is going to open. We just can't wait until headquarters decides to send a manageress and an accountant out here."

"I don't know about that," Mickey replied, shaking his head in bewilderment. "All I know is that it says right here that you can't open the club until the manageress and accountant get here."

Mickey had a one-track mind. He had a rule book, and he intended to follow it.

"Have you contacted headquarters and asked them when a manageress and accountant will be here?" Lisa asked.

"Yes, I have," Mickey said. "They told me they would send them out as soon as they are available."

"You mean they haven't even been hired yet? Well, they'd better get here pretty soon, because Lt. Winston said the club will be open by Friday, and that's only two days away. And I'm going to try to do it, accountant and manageress, or no."

"You're going to get into trouble," Mickey warned as he left.

True to his word, Lt. Winston was able to scrounge several dozen chairs and tables as well as stacks of coffee cups and a coffee urn. Sergeant Alexander delivered them to the club on Thursday, and then went to the town club to pick up the radio-phonograph and records.

Nick and Lisa had scrounged coal, sack by sack, until they had enough to keep the stoves going in the kitchen, the water hot, and to keep the fires burning in the snack bar stoves for at least one evening.

Lisa had contacted a sympathetic and kindly baker in a nearby village who agreed to deliver several thousand pastries to the club "on the cuff" because Lisa had no money to pay him. Neither had she received her ration points to assure his receiving more ingredients after his own supplies were gone.

The army PX agreed to turn the Coca-Cola ration for the base over to the club, and loaned Lisa money to make change on opening night. The Red Cross clubmobile girls who were based in Bury St. Edmunds, agreed to bring their clubmobile over to serve fresh hot doughnuts.

Finally, there was only one thing left to do by Thursday morning and that, Lisa thought, would not be too difficult. She would have Mickey drive her into Bury St. Edmunds where she hoped to get some help from the Ministry of Labour, and some ration points at the Ministry of Food. It seemed fairly simple.

Mickey let Lisa off at the offices of the Ministry of Labour, and promised to meet her at three that afternoon at the town club.

Lisa walked confidently up to the mild-mannered clerk at the Ministry counter, expecting to hire some women from their unemployment lists to help with the serving that evening. She soon learned that the British Ministry of Labour was not an employment agency. It was more like a Labour Gestapo which kept track of every man, woman and child in the country, and drafted those who were capable of working into the national labour force. Workers in England had no choice about where they would be sent, or what they would do. Often men would be transferred from their previous positions and sent to coal mines or factories far from their homes to fill war-time labour quotas.

The answer to Lisa's request was precise. "The American Red Cross does not have a priority with us, and therefore, we can not send anyone to help you."

Lisa sat down on a bench in the office pondering what to do next. She had a problem. The American Red Cross expected her to hire help on the English labour market. The Army had made it clear that she couldn't expect a military detail indefinitely. The Labour Ministry would not cooperate.

Lisa sat there puzzling over the problem for some time, until one of the typists in the office felt sorry for her, and came over. "You can't get help here," she said, "but perhaps the Women's Voluntary Services might be able to help you".

Lisa was willing to try. "Where would I find them?" she asked.

The girl gave directions, and Lisa left hurriedly. The Women's Voluntary Services office was located in two shabby rooms at the top of a rickety stairway above a store building several blocks up the street. At the head of the stairs Lisa opened the office door and was greeted by a middle-aged woman in a worn blue uniform who was sitting at a desk beside the door.

Lisa introduced herself and explained her mission. "I really must have help out there. I'm opening the club tomorrow evening and there will be several thousand men to serve, and of course it's impossible for me to handle them by myself."

The woman listened attentively. When Lisa stopped for breath, she spoke quietly. "I think I will be able to help you. Where do you plan to go from here?"

"I had intended to go to the Ministry of Food for ration points," Lisa answered uncertainly, fearful that if she left, the lady might change her mind about recruiting help.

But the lady was reassuring. "You go on there," she advised. "And when you've finished with your business there, ring me and I think I can promise that I will have help for you by then."

"Thank you very much," Lisa said gratefully. "Who shall I ask for when I call?"

"The Duchess of Grafton," the lady replied.

Lisa felt like Alice in Wonderland, but instead of exclaiming, "A real, live Duchess!" Lisa just said, "How do you do."

Although Lisa entered the Ministry of Food offices with her confidence in English Ministries shaken, nevertheless, she fared better there. Practically everything edible in England was rationed, and it was the obligation of the Ministry of Food to make certain that people and organizations should not receive more than their fair share.

This division of every loaf of bread in the Kingdom required a fantastic amount of paper work and red tape, such an incredible amount in fact, that at once Lisa knew it was hopeless for her to even attempt to understand the forms and procedures.

Later Lisa learned that the intricate negotiations required to obtain food ration points for an American Red Cross Aero Club was the province of the manageress and her superior, the "Kitchen Supervisor." These people were specially trained at headquarters to deal with the Ministries of Food and Supply. But Lisa didn't know this, and proceeded on her own.

Pressed for time as she was, she left the whole matter up to the clerk who attended her. "You make out the forms," she said. "Just give me my share for three thousand men."

The clerk, no doubt relieved that Lisa had no intention of bargaining with her, went to work filling out the forms. Two hours later, the clerk had finished, and Lisa was in receipt of a handful of ration point books. She then called the Duchess, who to her great joy told her there were two civilian women who would be at the club to help the next evening at six o'clock.

When Mickey and Lisa returned to the base, they walked into the club and found Harold Cross there. He had come to deliver a message from Andy. "Andy won't be able to keep his date with you tonight." Harold said. "I told him I would act as a liaison between you two, because there will be times when he has to change his plans."

"Thank you very much," Lisa said sincerely. "I am grateful to you for understanding how it is."

"It's my pleasure to be of help," Harold said.

Harold seemed so sincere that Lisa thought she must have been mistaken about him. Really he was a kind and thoughtful man.

The next morning Lisa woke early. It was opening day for the club, There was only one more chore in town. Lisa was to go on a shopping spree with her new ration point cards. Mickey agreed to drive her into town and to wait for her at the town club while she purchased sausage meat which was mostly cereal disguised as meat and seasoned with an intriguing combination of herbs, and buns with mustard, which Lisa hoped would pass muster as an English version of an American hamburger.

It was almost three when Lisa had finished her shopping which she had stored at the Town Club. Mickey was there as he had promised he would be. But sometime during the hours since he had left Lisa at the grocer's, Mickey had been bitten by the love bug. The object of his affections was an attractive red-headed civilian nurse from the village hospital by the name of Elaine. Mickey and Elaine had made plans to pick heather on the moors several miles out of town. Lisa wouldn't have objected to that, except they expected to go flower-picking right then and there, and Lisa was to go along and wait for them.

Lisa objected vehemently. "I haven't got time to pick heather," she said. "The club opens at six o'clock, and I still have lots to do. Why don't you drive me out to the field, and let me out; then you two can drive back and pick heather all night if you want to?"

But Mickey had made up his mind. "No," he said firmly. "No, I can't do that. Elaine has to report for work at five, and we wouldn't have time. I promised her I would help her pick heather to cheer her patients at the hospital."

For the next hour and a half, Lisa sulked in the Crosley, which was parked beside a country lane, while Mickey and his English lassie traipsed gaily over the moors in search of heather.

By the time Mickey deposited Elaine and her flowers at the hospital and had driven the three miles to the base, it was almost six, and soldiers were lined up a full city block in front of the club. Lisa hurried into the club, and found everything in readiness.

Nick...loyal, faithful, good Nick, had made coffee in the large urns. The Red Cross Clubmobile girls were there with trays of doughnuts they had made especially for the occasion, and the two English volunteers were at the counters arranging doughnuts and pastries, and pouring coffee into cups that Lt. Winston had borrowed from the mess hall. The pot-bellied stoves had been lit, and the big dining room was warm and comfortable. Lt. Winston was there, too, overseeing everything, and waiting impatiently for Lisa to show up.

It was with a light heart that Lisa opened the door and invited the soldiers into the club. She thought they would be pleased because so much had been accomplished in such a short time. But they liked the NAAFI better, and said so. The NAAFI, they said, served fish and chips, and beer, which obviously was more to their liking than Coca-Cola, coffee, sausage hamburgers, sweets, and doughnuts.

It was a dismal start to a career as the director of an American Red Cross Aero Club.

Lt. Winston tried to be encouraging. "I have plans for this club," he said. "The enlisted men will change their minds soon."

Lisa was skeptical. But shortly she, too, would change her mind. Lt. Winston meant what he said.

The club closed at eleven o'clock, and when Lt. Winston and all of the GIs had left, Lisa thanked the volunteers and the Doughnut Dollies of the Clubmobile Corps. When they, too, had departed, she dropped exhausted into a chair.

Nick stood looking at her sympathetically. Lisa was over-whelmed with gratitude towards him. "Nick," she said, "I don't know what I'd do without you. Honestly, I don't."

Nick was embarrassed. He tried to say what was in his mind. "It will get better, Miss Lisa," he managed. "I'll work hard to make it better."

"I know you will," Lisa said.

At that moment there was a knock on the door. Lisa rose and walked down the hall to the door. It was Andy. He was smiling, but he looked tired, and Lisa was shocked to see stress lines on his face that had not been there two days before. "Come in Andy," Lisa said. "I'll pour you a cup of coffee. You look tired."

When they returned to the kitchen Nick had gone, and they were alone.

"Harold Cross said you couldn't come tonight, but I'm glad you made it. Was it bad?" Lisa asked, as she poured the coffee.

"Yes," Andy replied. "We lost two planes today. But I don't want to talk about that. I came to ask you to a dance next Saturday evening at the Eighth Army headquarters at Elvidon Hall. We're invited."

Lisa hesitated, "I don't know. I've just opened the club, and Lt. Winston..."

"Lt. Winston will be at the dance, so he can't complain about you. You can get someone to take over for one night, surely."

"Of course I can. I would love to go to the dance with you Andy. But I don't have a party dress, you know. I'll have to wear my uniform. We were told that we should not bring formal attire because it would cause women in war-torn countries to be envious of us."

"You will look beautiful to me whatever you wear," Andy said as he put his arms around her. But this is to be a formal affair and if you'd really like to wear a party dress I know where you can get one. There's a very nice dress shop in Bury St. Edmunds, and you don't need ration cards for party dresses. It will be a gift from me to you... to let you know how much I love you."

"You certainly do get around. How do you know about dress shops and party dresses?"

Andy grinned. "Well you know I was here a while before you arrived, and there were a few parties and such. But that's all behind me now, so let me enjoy doing whatever I can do for you. You do a lot to make me happy, and I'd like to return the favor"

"I accept your kind offer," Lisa said. "If you tell me where the shop is located, I'll go shopping tomorrow. I really would feel better if I were dressed for the occasion."

As they kissed good-night Lisa felt the thrill of anticipation of a good time to come. Nevertheless, she knew that tomorrow would bring more danger and more anxious waiting. It was a burden she would bear every day until there was peace again, and that would be a long time.

CHAPTER 13

A TERRIBLE DAY

When Lisa entered the club early in the morning she saw a large truck driving into the courtyard, and the driver began unloading dozens of packing boxes.

Nick and Lisa started opening the boxes immediately, and there it was... all the equipment they'd been needing for days. They unwrapped pots, pans, cooking utensils, dishes and coffee urns. Lisa couldn't imagine what kind geni had smiled down upon her efforts, until she saw an inconspicuous address label which read: 'Ministry of Works.'

"God Bless the Ministry of Works," she said.

Mickey drove into the courtyard while Nick and Lisa were in the process of opening packages. He was beaming. "I told you equipment would arrive," he said.

Lisa's estimation of the Ministry of Works increased as time went on. Within the next few weeks, the Ministry of Works and the American Red Cross headquarters had sent chairs, tables, sofas, a radio-phonograph, records, playing cards, pencils, stationery, the inevitable doughnut making machine with doughnut mixture and lard, and three thousand books that had been donated by people at home.

Also Lisa learned that before her arrival, the London headquarters had sent an interior decorator to the club, who had ordered drapes for all the windows, furniture for all the rooms, and complete equipment for the kitchen. Orders for all of these things had been placed through the Ministry of Works where they were filled, and the merchandise shipped when and if it became available. The cost was charged to the American side of Lend-Lease, an unbelievably wonderful arrangement where everybody got everything for nothing. The British ordered what they wanted from America, the Americans took whatever they needed from the British, and no-one had to pay because everyone knew that, in the end, it would all be cancelled off even all around.

Lisa was so happy and excited over the arrival of the truck that she had temporarily forgotten that this was a mission day. She had known instinctively when Andy left the evening before that he would be on a mission, and she knew by the silence in the area this morning that the planes were flying over enemy territory. Lisa began to feel the tension rising, as she and everyone else on the base waited for the sound of returning planes.

It was almost noon when Lisa heard the first planes arriving, and then she was startled by the sound of a plane in trouble, flying low and sputtering and coming closer until she thought surely it would slam into the club. Nick, too, recognized the danger, and they both ran outside where they saw parachutes coming down, and watched the plane dive into the ground and burst into flames not thirty feet away.

Lisa heard someone say, "It's Lt. Larry Aronson." and that was the last Lisa remembered. The next thing she knew, she was in her quarters lying on her cot underneath a blanket. The clubmobile girls, Esther and Ann, were knocking on her door, asking her if she was O.K.

"Yes, I'm all right," she answered. "But I don't remember coming in here."

"Lt. Winston brought you in here," Esther answered. " He said he thought you were in shock, and he wants to know if you're all right."

"Tell him I'm all right, and I'll be out in a minute. We have to get word to Elsa, and I want to be the one to tell her."

"We'll tell Lt. Winston," Esther said.

Lisa arose, washed her face, applied make-up, combed her hair and put on a clean blouse. Once again she was on automatic, doing what she had to do without thinking. There was only one thought in her mind. She had to get to Elsa as soon as she could.

When Lisa entered the club, a small crowd was there. Lt. Winston, Harold Cross, Esther, Ann, and several soldiers were drinking coffee in the dining area, and Nick was in the kitchen serving everyone. Lisa walked over to Lt. Winston. "Is there any way you can take me to Elsa's base?" she asked.

"Yes of course I can," he said."I've already ordered a car, and we'll leave right away."

When Lt. Winston and Lisa arrived at Elsa's club, they found Elsa sitting alone in the kitchen. "I know why you've come," she said. "Something has happened to Larry."

Lisa walked over and put her hand on Elsa's shoulder. "You have to be brave, Elsa."

"I know," Elsa said. "But I don't have to stay here and take more of this. I'm leaving this place. This is some kind of a hell-hole where they're killing our best men. Our country can't make it if we keep on killing men like Larry. I don't want to be a part of it any longer."

Lisa put her arm around Elsa's shoulder, and spoke quietly to her: "Remember Elsa, what you said to me when I heard about Steve? You told me that I had a job to do. Remember?"

Elsa looked up, and nodded as comprehension slowly dawned. "Yes, I remember," she said. "And you did it. I don't know if I can, but I guess I can try."

Lisa was relieved. She knew that Elsa would be O.K. It would take time, but she would make it.

"I think you should come back with me and Lt. Winston. You shouldn't be alone tonight, and the extra bed is still in my quarters," Lisa said.

Elsa nodded. "Yes, I want to be with you tonight. I'll get my things together."

Elsa stayed with Lisa for three days, working hard in the kitchen, washing dishes, cleaning counters and standing over the stove frying sausage for hamburgers during the evening rush hours. Never once did Lisa see Elsa cry, not even when they were alone in the quarters discussing everything and everyone except Larry.

Wednesday morning Lisa asked Elsa if she would like to drive into Bury St. Edmunds. Lisa was planning to look up the dress shop that Andy had told her about, and she was hesitant about asking Elsa to join her because she thought Elsa was not in a mood to be excited about anyone buying a dress for a fancy military ball. But Elsa's reply was a surprise. "Of course I'd like to go," she said."You know I love clothes, and maybe I can find a dress for myself." Then she added wistfully: "But I don't know where I'd wear it."

Lisa and Elsa easily located the dress shop from directions that Andy had given them. A wonderfully considerate English saleswoman greeted them and listened to Lisa's plea for a party dress. Then the saleslady rummaged about in a cluttered closet, and emerged with a carton of pre-war formals, from which Lisa selected a blue taffeta gown that was as lovely as any she had left at home. Andy was right. It was a super dress shop, and party dresses did not require coupons. Lisa was delighted. Elsa sadly did not try on a dress for herself. "I won't be going to any dances for a while," she said.

That evening Elsa told Lisa that she was ready to return to her base. "It has helped me to be here and to learn that Larry died heroically," she said. "It was like him to bail the crew out, and then fly the plane into the ground to save others. I hope they will honor him with a medal."

"I'm sure they will. Maybe the medal of honor. He certainly deserves it. Andy is off tonight, and we'll take you back to your base."

It was Saturday night, and Lisa, dressed in her lovely new blue taffeta gown, was looking forward to an exciting evening. She was not disappointed. Andy knocked on her door, and she opened it to see Andy, in his dress uniform with medals and braid, and silver wings on his chest. Lisa thought he was the best looking man she had ever seen. Andy also was pleased. "You look absolutely beautiful, Lisa," he said.

Elvidon Hall was a sixty-room castle with winding staircases, magnificent marble halls, and central heating. The ball was a gala affair, reminiscent of pre-war days when members of royalty danced there. An excellent orchestra was playing the latest dance tunes, and the great hall was brilliant with army brass, titled ladies and celebrities who were dancing with American army officers. But the biggest surprise of all for Lisa occurred when she and Andy entered the big dance hall, and saw Elsa there. Elsa was dancing with a young air force officer, and she was wearing her tight-fitting above-the-knees black sequin dress, black silk hosiery and high-heeled black shoes, and she was smiling.

When Elsa saw Lisa and Andy, she stopped dancing and ran up to Lisa and hugged her. "I'm so glad you're here, Lisa," she said. "I want you to meet Lt. Sampson. He's the special service officer on my base, and he's been very kind and helpful to me in getting the club going."

"If it's like my club, I'm sure Elsa is grateful for your help," Lisa said to Lt. Sampson. "And I want you to meet Lt. Andy Thompson who has been kind and helpful to me."

When Elsa and Lt. Sampson returned to the dance floor, Andy turned to Lisa and she felt a thrill of anticipation as he took her in his arms and led her in the first dance they had ever danced together. Lisa was not disappointed. Andy was a beautiful and confident dancer, and she knew this evening was the beginning of many happy times they would share together on a dance floor.

But when the music stopped, Lisa noted that Andy was looking across the room at Elsa and Lt. Sampson, and he was frowning. "She didn't take long getting over Larry," he said bitterly.

"She's not over Larry," Lisa demurred. "She may be smiling, but her eyes are sad, and her heart is aching. She's just doing her job."

"I'm sorry I said that," Andy apologized. "Of course you're right, but how did you know?"

"I just know," Lisa said. "But now let's dance. It's going to be a wonderful evening." And it was!

Lt. Winston was there with a lovely young English girl from the town, and very soon came over to exchange partners with Andy, which started a whirl of exchanges. Lisa, to her surprise danced with several airmen who could do the jitterbug steps. It was an unexpected thrill for Lisa who like many others, had become a jitterbug enthusiast, and she had not danced the jitterbug since the show on the Rangitata.

Andy, too, was impressed. "You'll have to teach me how to do that," he said to Lisa.

"I'll be delighted," Lisa promised. "You won't have any trouble learning because you're already a wonderful dancer. It will be fun. And if you're nice to Elsa, she'll teach you how to do the rhumba. Look at what she's doing now."

True enough, Elsa was attracting the attention of every man in the room, twirling her hips and shaking her shoulders and smiling as if she were enjoying herself. As usual, Elsa was the belle of the ball. Only Lisa knew that Elsa was crying inside.

CHAPTER 14

THE MINISTRY OF AIR

For Lisa the Ministry of Air was the most difficult of all of the British ministries. It was always standing between her and her efforts to carry out directives from American Red Cross headquarters in London. Apparently the American Red Cross and the Air Ministry had not come to an understanding, or perhaps they hadn't even met, because each went its own way, completely oblivious of the other. As a result, directives would come down from Red Cross headquarters, only to be blocked by Air Ministry officials.

One painful example of the difficulties such a misunderstanding caused for Lisa was the matter of building two brick fireplaces, one in the lounge room, the other in the library. This suggestion came to Lisa in the form of a directive from Red Cross headquarters.

"Build fireplaces?" Lisa asked when Mickey showed her the directive.

"That's what the directive says," Mickey answered.

"Sure," Lisa agreed, trying to be funny, but not feeling that way at all. "I'll just keep piling one brick on top of another with a hole in the middle, until I reach the roof. It ought to be easy."

But Mickey was serious. "You'll have to do it," he said. "It says so, right here. Besides, all of the other club directors are building fireplaces."

That did it. "All right," Lisa said. "If the other club directors can do impossible things, I can too."

Armed with the Red Cross directive, Lisa called on Mr. Randall, the Clerk of the Works, and asked him to order mortar and bricks for two large fireplaces.

Mr. Randall shook his head. "It cawn't be done," he said.

Mr. Randall's refusal alarmed Lisa, and in spite of what must have been a shocking resemblance to Mickey, she showed him the directive. Pointing to the word 'fireplaces' she said: "You see, it says right here that I should have fireplaces built in the lounge and library."

Mr. Randall, however, was not as impressed with the directive as Lisa had thought he would be. "It cawn't be done," he insisted. "I'd like to do it for you if I could, but the regulations of the Air Ministry will not permit altering the structure of any of the buildings without permission. There's nothing I can do about it."

Then, shifting his ever-present pipe to the other side of his mouth, he added, with just a touch of irritation: "The RAF doesn't require fireplaces in their canteens, and I'm sure the Ministry will take a dim view of building them for the Yanks."

Lisa quickly reversed her original opinion of Mr. Randall as a jolly man who wanted to help, and unreasonably decided he was petty and envious and just didn't want the American soldiers to have fireplaces in their club. Lisa, like so many other Americans, had little comprehension of the shortage difficulties that the British were suffering. Also, Lisa assumed that the American Red Cross headquarters would not send out a directive of that kind without first clearing it through the Air Ministry. Lisa decided that if the GIs on the other bases were to have fireplaces, the men on her base would have them, too.

As was becoming her custom in time of difficulty, Lisa turned to Lt. Winston.

"I think it's a fine idea to build fireplaces in the club," Lt. Winston said. "I should have thought of that myself."

That afternoon, accompanied by Lt. Winston and Mickey, Lisa made a trip to the brickyard in Bury St. Edmunds. There, the owner of the yard conferred with Lt. Winston and Mickey, and together they computed the number of bricks that would be needed. Lisa bought the bricks "on the cuff," and made arrangements to have them delivered to the club.

Lt. Winston located a former building contractor and several brick-layers amongst the military personnel on the base, and persuaded the Colonel to assign them to work at the club. Soon the fireplaces were well on the way to becoming realities.

But Mr. Randall, with what must have been considerable astonishment, noted that the sides of two of his buildings were being torn out to make way for fireplaces, and he must have decided that the situation was beyond his control, because he called in his chief, Mr. Leaven, district head of the Air Ministry, whose offices were at Air Ministry headquarters in Cambridge.

Lisa thought it was unfair of Mr. Randall to call in such auspicious reinforcements without warning her in advance so that she could call for help, too...the American Red Cross Commissioner or somebody. But Lisa realized that he had his directives, just as she had hers.

Mr. Leaven arrived, accompanied by two of his subordinates. At the base they were joined by Mr. Randall and his chief engineer, and the American quartermaster officer, and all six of them called on Lt. Winston at his office.

After the delegation had explained it's mission, Lt. Winston retired to another room to call Lisa. "A delegation of Air Ministry officials from Cambridge will be coming to see you," he said. "They want to know where you got authority to tear out the ends of those buildings."

"When will they be here?" Lisa asked.

"In a few minutes. And Lisa," Lt Winston added, "perhaps you'd better let me handle this."

"All right," Lisa agreed, "but I don't know what they're so upset about. We're not planning to leave holes in their precious buildings."

"Maybe you'd better leave this to me," Lt. Winston repeated, and Lisa noted the concern in his voice.

Lisa knew that the situation must be serious, so she rushed into the kitchen to put the hot water kettle on the stove to boil water for tea. Already, she had learned the magic powers of a cup of tea in the hands of an Englishman.

Mr. Randall led the group into Lisa's little office, and she knew at once that the chief was Mr. Leaven. He was by far the most distinguished man in the group. He stood with great dignity... tall and ram-rod straight. His most distinguishing feature however, was his mustache, which was waxed and rolled, and stood straight out from each side of his upper lip. Mr. Leaven was very cool, which is the nearest any Englishman ever comes to appearing angry. He sat gingerly on the chair that Mr. Randall pushed towards him.

When the bustle of introductions was over and everyone was seated, Lisa poured tea, and they all engaged in a polite discussion of the weather. Finally, Mr. Leaven with great deliberation, set his cup and saucer on the desk, sat even straighter in his chair, and came to the point of his visit.

"Now about those walls," he said, looking directly at Lisa. "Mr. Randall informs me that you have not obtained proper authority to alter from the Ministry of Air. Is this correct?"

"Yes," Lisa answered meekly. "I'm afraid it is."

"Mr. Randall also informs me that you have chosen to proceed without his permission, even though he discussed the matter with you previously. Is this also correct?"

"Yes. That's true too."

"Would you mind telling me why it is so important that you have fireplaces in this club?" Mr. Leaven inquired.

Lisa spoke haltingly..."Well, the other Aero Clubs are building fireplaces, but mostly, I'm planning to have a grand opening party, and I wanted the club to look nice."

Mr. Leaven interrupted: "You must realize that you are guilty of a criminal offense."

"What?" Lt. Winston interjected.

Lisa wanted to tell Lt. Winston not to get excited, because she was sure it wouldn't be cricket for the Air Ministry to incarcerate a Red Cross girl in an English jail. It would be bad for Anglo-American relations.

Mr. Leaven, too, was quite aware that sending Lisa to jail was out of the question, and he hastened to add: "This doesn't necessarily mean that you will be sent to jail, but you might be liable to a heavy fine. Five hundred pounds, perhaps."

"Heavens!" This time it was Lisa who exclaimed. Lisa knew that while it might not be logical for the Air Ministry to send her to jail, it was quite conceivable that it might impose a fine on the American Red Cross for her transgression of British law.

Lisa was frightened, so frightened that she couldn't think of a thing to say in defense. Her self-confidence was completely shattered. For a time no one spoke, and during the tense silence, Mr. Leaven, in an unhurried and precise way, stood up straight as if he were standing at attention. "I say," he said, "since so much devastation has been created already, I suppose you must continue, but in the future I expect you to obtain proper authority for your projects."

"Yes Sir, I will," Lisa promised.

Mr. Leaven stood straighter and spoke again to Lisa: "I will drop all charges against you on one condition."

"And what is that condition?"

"That you invite me to your party."

Lisa smiled, and stood to shake Mr. Leaven's hand. "You're invited," she said.

CHAPTER 15

THE MINISTRY OF LABOUR

Of all the problems that weighed heavily on the mind of a Red Cross Aero Club Director in England, and probably the most urgent, was the problem of hiring help to staff the club.

Lisa soon learned that the American Red Cross did not have a priority with the Ministry of Labour which had jurisdiction in this area. However, although exceedingly difficult, it was not an impossible problem. The Ministry maintained jurisdiction only over women who were over fifteen years of age, or under sixty. Anyone above or below that age bracket, or any housewife with children, could work when, where, and if they pleased.

Whenever Lisa could find time, she biked about through the neighboring farms and villages, searching for people who were outside the jurisdiction of the Ministry of Labour, and who could be persuaded to work in a Yank canteen.

It took much persuasion and an exasperating amount of time, because the rural English people were suspicious of Americans and no one ever promised to come right away. However, she hired one young girl, and then another, and after a while it was easier. Once they learned that Americans didn't scalp Englishmen and roast them over an open fire, they seemed to enjoy working on an American airfield.

Since the only people Lisa could hire by this method were very young country girls or very old housewives, and since they could only clean and serve, the most urgent problem was finding at least two cooks capable of cooking for several thousand men.

Lisa's first hope for finding a cook came from one of the GIs Lt. Winston had detailed to work on the redecorating of the club rooms. He told Lisa that a civilian workmen's canteen nearby was closing, and the cook there would be out of work.

"But that doesn't do me any good," Lisa said. "She will have to report back to the Ministry of Labour, and they won't let me have anyone unless they're under fifteen or over sixty, or unless they have children."

"She has some kids," he said. "Several of them in fact, and all without a name."

"Hmmmmm-mm," Lisa murmured, not thinking of the same thing he was. Lisa threw off her muslin apron, called to Nick to watch the club while she biked to a nearby canteen to hire a cook.

Lisa talked with the cook, who said her name was Jane, while Jane was preparing a meal on an evil-smelling oil stove at the canteen. Lisa felt only joy, and no qualms at all, when the cook agreed to her proposal. Neither Lisa nor the cook mentioned the Ministry of Labour.

Jane was a mousy girl, frail and unkempt, and although still young, she was already stooped from hard work. But Jane was a Godsend to Lisa when she immediately took over the coffee-making detail, and learned quickly how to make hundreds of doughnuts and sandwiches each day. Jane even found time to help Lisa fry hamburgers which they made from "ration-free" sausage meal. They mixed the meal with leaks, doused it with mustard sauce, and served it on a dark-bread bun. These "hamburgers" were a favorite of the G.I.'s and no matter how fast Jane and Lisa made them, they could never keep up with the demand. It was a mystery to Lisa why the hamburgers were so popular. Even the English people, accustomed as they were to ersatz products, joked about the ration-free sausage meal. They said that the greatest hero of the war would turn out to be an under-sized Scottish pig who furnished sausage for all of England throughout the war.

Everything was proceeding fairly well with the new cook and Lisa was grateful that she had found her. But the Ministry of Labour was on its toes and up on its regulations, because barely a week had passed when Lisa received a letter from the Ministry. The letter stated: "You have hired a cook without proper authority from the Ministry of Labour, and therefore you are subject to a prison sentence, and or a fine not exceeding five hundred pounds."

"Ye Gods!' Lisa exclaimed to Nick when she read it. "Every time I turn around in this country, I put my foot in a jail door."

"Will they put you in jail?" Nick asked, alarmed.

"No" Lisa answered. "I think they just like to worry me with these jail threats."

Nick looked relieved, but uncomprehending, as he turned back to his sweeping. Lisa picked up the phone to call the motor pool for a jeep to take her to the offices of the Labour Ministry in Bury St. Edmunds.

The manager was a kindly man who was apologetic as he explained that the letter really didn't mean what it said.

"It's just regulation to send a letter like this when someone has broken a Ministry rule," he explained.

"But I didn't think I broke one," Lisa protested. "My understanding was that I could hire women with children, and my cook has three."

"Yes, but your cook has no husband," the manager explained gently, as if Lisa were a child who could not be expected to know the Ministry's uncompromising attitude toward such carelessness.

"I think I understand," Lisa said. "Illegitimate children don't count...but what I'd like to know is whether or not I can keep her, even though she doesn't have a husband?"

"I think that might be arranged," the manager agreed uncertainly, "but she must register at the Ministry within the next few days."

"Oh, she'll register all right", Lisa promised, "and thank you very much for letting me keep her."

Lisa was pleased and relieved. She felt she was beginning to make progress getting the club into efficient shape, and maybe finding a little time for herself. She and Andy were able to see one another very irregularly, and usually only for a cup of coffee and a snack in the kitchen after the club had closed.

Even the evening bike rides that they had enjoyed had been cancelled because Lisa always had to be at the club preparing for the evening rush. During the morning hours she had to be in town shopping for provisions. Lisa was trying to cram two days' work into one, and she knew she couldn't do it for long, and she knew it wasn't fair to Andy. Andy was not driving into town with the other fliers for dates and recreation on his free nights. He was just waiting for Lisa, and she knew that for his sake, as well as her own, she had to have help, and soon.

Because of the urgency of her situation, Lisa was not prepared for the jolt she received from Mickey when she entered the kitchen. Mickey was standing there with a rule book in his hand. "Well," he said, as if he were pleased with himself, "I fired your cook."

"You what?" Lisa exclaimed, not daring to believe her ears.

"I fired your cook," he said again.

"But who's cooking tonight?" Lisa asked."Who's making the coffee and the sandwiches and doughnuts?"

"That's your job."

"But why? Why on earth did you do a thing like that?"

Lisa was angry. She had to bite her tongue to keep from screaming at Mickey, but she managed a measured tone when she spoke to him again. "Mickey," she said. "If it's my job, I must get busy because the club will open in an hour. And while I'm cooking you are to get into your little 'ol Crosley and you're going to drive into the village and hire Jane again. And if you're worried about your stupid rule book, you can quit worrying because I have permission from the Ministry of Labour to keep Jane even if she has three illegitimate children."

Mickey looked puzzled. "It said in the rule book..."

"I don't care about the rule book, just get Jane back."

"All right, all right. I'll get Jane back, but you're going to get in trouble." Mickey warned as he turned towards the door.

It had been a long day for Lisa when she finally closed the club at eleven P.M. But at least Mickey had returned and had informed her that Jane would be back on the job the next day. She had just finished talking with him and was starting to lock the door when Andy arrived. She noted that Andy looked very tired. The stress lines were back, and he seemed sad. "Are you all right?" Lisa asked.

"I'm O.K." he replied."It was just a bad day."

"I'm sorry."

"I would like to talk to you for a few minutes. How about a cup of coffee?"

"Of course," Lisa said as she turned to fill a cup from the coffee urn, and placed it before Andy on the counter. "I'm ready to talk, or hug, or kiss."

Andy smiled. "You have a way of breaking the tension," he said as he took Lisa in his arms and kissed her. "I came over here tonight to ask you if I've told you lately that I love you?"

"Not lately," Lisa said. "We've both been too busy for that kind of nonsense."

"It isn't nonsense," Andy said. "It's real. I've come over to ask you to marry me."

It was too much for Lisa. She sat down on a stool and put her head on the counter, and she was crying. Andy put his arm across her shoulder.

"Please don't cry Lisa," he said. "I know this isn't the most romantic place in the world to ask for a girl's hand in marriage, but it's the only place we have, and we don't have much time."

Lisa lifted her head and looked at him through her tears. She was completely confused. "What do you mean we don't have much time?' she asked. "Do you mean we should get married here...right now, in England?"

"Why not?" Andy replied, as he wiped her tears away with a napkin. "English girls are getting married here all the time."

"I know, but I'm not an English girl, and I don't know how they do it, and I have to get ready for the opening party for the club, and the maintenance crews want me to help them stage a dance and party in town, and I don't know how I can find time to get married just now."

"I'll take care of the details," Andy said. "I've already talked to the Colonel, and the Chaplain and they will help."

"You've talked to the Colonel and the Chaplain, and you don't know yet if I will say yes?"

"I take my chances."

"You certainly do. But I want to know what's the hurry? I didn't even know you were thinking of such a thing."

"I told you I was thinking of some things about you and me, and I've been thinking about something else. You know I'm not exactly in a risk free job. I don't mind that so much, but I think all men dislike the idea of checking out of this life without leaving an heir to live after them."

Lisa's eyes were wide with shock. "You mean I should have a baby here...in England?"

"Lots of English girls are having babies here every day."

"But I'm not an English girl and I wouldn't have the foggiest notion of what I would do with a baby here, and is that the reason you want to marry me?"

A pained expression flashed across Andy's face, and he put his hands on the counter and bowed his head. "How could you think such a thing? If that were all, I don't think it would be too difficult. There are lots of English girls about, but I happen to be in love with you, and I don't want just anybody to be the mother of a child of mine. Surely, you must know that."

"I'm sorry Andy. Of course I know that. It's just that it's been a long, hard day for me, and a much harder day for you. We should talk about this later."

"The way things are going, later may be too late. But I understand. I should have prepared you for all of this. It must have been a shock if you've never thought of it."

"Of course I've thought of it, but not here...in England."

"I'll be free tomorrow, and perhaps we can meet in town for lunch at the Angel Hotel"

"I'll be there." Lisa said. "And Andy, I do love you."

Andy smiled as he took Lisa in his arms. "I think everything's going to be O.K." he said.

CHAPTER 16

MAKING PLANS

Lisa woke up in a happy mood. She had a good night's sleep. After Andy left she immediately went to bed and slept straight through until morning. It was one of the rare nights when the Tanoy loudspeaker did not awaken her to warn that enemy planes were overhead. Also Lisa knew that Andy would not be flying this day because he had said he would meet her at noon at the Angel Hotel. Surely it would be a wonderful day, and Lisa was looking forward to an exciting lunch meeting with Andy. She was thinking of what she and Andy would be talking about and what she would say. Somehow, this morning the idea of marriage and even a baby did not seem as startlingly impossible as it had seemed the night before.

It was with a light heart that Lisa entered the kitchen and sat down for a cup of coffee which Nick, dear Nick, had prepared for her.

"The maintenance crew chief was here a while ago," Nick said. "He wants to know if you've had time to get ration coupons for the dance in town on Saturday night."

"I'm planning to do that today," Lisa replied. "As a matter of fact, I'm leaving for town right away. I have a lot to do today. If the sergeant comes in again while I'm gone, tell him I've already arranged to serve doughnuts, and I'll get rations for snacks. Also tell him I've contacted several bases where Land Army girls and WAAFs are stationed, and I've arranged transportation for them to attend the dance. He will be pleased."

"You'd better have breakfast before you leave."

Lisa smiled. "You must stop worrying about me, Nick...I'll just have coffee and a doughnut. That's all I want. I'm having lunch in town at the Angel Hotel today."

Mickey came early to drive Lisa into town as he had promised, and he stayed with her while she completed her errands at the Ministry of Food for extra ration cards for the party, and for snack food for the club which they bought at the green grocer's and the meat market. Then Mickey obligingly drove Lisa to the Angel Hotel to meet Andy, and offered to take her supplies back to the base. It was indeed a wonderful day, and Mickey was being unusually cooperative. Lisa entered the hotel Lobby and saw Andy standing there waiting for her with outstretched arms and a welcoming smile.

Andy had reserved the table where they first met and had ordered gin and bitters for two. When the waiter had served them, Andy proposed a simple toast: "To us."

Lisa smiled and as they clicked their glasses, she repeated after him: "To us."

"You mean it?" he asked.

Lisa nodded, and Andy leaned over and kissed her in front of a staring audience of curious diners.

During the luncheon, Lisa and Andy made their plans. It seemed so simple. They would set the wedding date for as soon as possible after the official opening of the club which Lisa estimated would take place within a month. When they were able to set the exact date, Andy would contact the church officials of the little church on the outskirts of the base, and would also take care of the wedding license and military requirements, including permission for a few days off for a honeymoon. "All you will have to do is be there," he told Lisa.

"I'll be there." she promised.

As Lisa and Andy rode back to the base in the military command car, the sun appeared for the first time in days. It was shining on the hoarfrost that covered the hedge rows like a glistening blanket. Lisa thought the sun was shining especially for her, and her spirits were soaring. Andy had his arm around Lisa as they sat in the back seat of the command car. Lisa noted that it was the first time they had not sat straight upright, observing army protocol. "Are you concerned that the C.O. might see us cuddling like this?" she asked Andy.

"No," he answered, "The Colonel already knows about us, and he'll be pleased."

When the command car reached the base, Andy directed the driver to let Lisa off at the club, and to drive him on to his quarters. "I won't be able to have coffee with you after the club closes tonight," he said. "I have orders to be in early."

"I understand," Lisa said. Indeed, she did understand. By now she was fully aware of the routine, and she knew Andy would be on a mission the next morning, and she would be waiting for the sound of planes returning, and would be anxiously watching for Harold Cross to report to her.

CHAPTER 17

EVERYTHING GOES WRONG

It was Friday, the day before the maintenance crews' dance in town. Andy was on a mission, and Lisa, as usual, was anxiously waiting for Harold Cross to report. She was greatly relieved when Harold Cross told her that Andy had returned and was all right.

Once again, however, planes had been lost, and there was a hesitancy in the way Harold Cross reported to her, as if he were unsure about how much he should tell her. Obviously, the danger was becoming greater, and Harold Cross was not telling Lisa everything he knew.

That evening after the club had closed, Andy knocked on the door. Lisa opened the door and was shocked when she saw him. He looked exhausted, and sad, and the stress lines were in his face again. Lisa knew why Harold Cross seemed reluctant to tell her much about Andy that morning.

"Are you all right?" she asked.

"Yes," but it has been a rough day. We were attacked by two fighter planes and I lost three men. Everyone except my bombardier, Jim Jackson, and I were wounded. The plane was damaged, and I won't be flying missions again until the plane has been repaired and I've been assigned a new crew. It's hell out there, Lisa."

"I know it is," Lisa said, "and you can't take much more of it. Maybe you can get a leave for a day or two. Sometimes that helps."

"That's what I want to tell you," Andy said. "Jim and I thought we would take a couple of days off, and go to London. You have the dance in town tomorrow night, and we'll be back Monday. I'll see you then."

"That's wonderful," Lisa said. "I hope you have a good time, but not too good. I've got enough problems already without worrying about you and some glamorous English gal."

Andy smiled. "You haven't got any worries about me on that score."

Saturday, the day of the maintenance crew's ball, finally dawned. Lisa was pleased that everything seemed to be in order. A GI detail had been sent to the hall the day before to decorate with Petty Girl posters and tables were ready for doughnuts, snacks and coffee. Jane and Lisa were busy all morning making fresh doughnuts and snacks and waiting for the planes to return from a mission. Andy was in London so Lisa was not worrying about him that day, but like everyone else on the base, she was anxiously waiting for the first sound of returning planes.

Lisa thought all of the men who flew in the B-26 bombers must be especially brave men. The B-26 was a "hot ship" that flew as fast as a fighter plane and was dangerous to fly. When it came in for a landing, it scorched onto the runway at a 130 mile per hour clip that had caused many crack-ups. Many men, it was said, had been killed learning to fly the B-26 on training bases and during test flights.

Hoping to evade German radar, the pilots flew the B-26 at a low level, just above the tree tops, even though it was a bomber, designed to fly much higher. The townspeople around the base were annoyed and critical of this. They thought the American pilots were show-offs, who buzzed the town just to frighten the populace. But this was not the case. The pilots were flying low in training for low-flying bombing missions over Germany.

The crews would sometimes discuss the B-26 bomber in the club. They were not as enthusiastic about it as the pilots seemed to be. They said that, like a bumble bee, the plane's body was too big for its wing-spread, and logically, it couldn't fly at all. They said that when the plane made its first test flight at the Glenn Martin plant, the assembly crews were on the line betting that it wouldn't lift off the ground.

Officially, the B-26 bomber was known as the "Martin Marauder," but the crews had other names for it. They called it the "Flying Prostitute" because it had no visible means of support, the "Widow Maker," and most descriptively, "B-dash-crash."

Everyone agreed that the B-26 was a dangerous plane to fly.

This Saturday, Lisa, like everyone else, began to worry when the noon hour passed and she had heard nothing of the planes on mission. Finally she saw Harold Cross enter the club. She knew immediately by the grim set of his jaw that the news was bad. "They won't be back," he said.

"None of them?"Lisa asked.

"None," he answered. "The base has been restricted, and all leaves have been cancelled."

"How many were lost?"

"Ten planes. Eighty men."

"That's terrible. What will we do about the dance tonight?" Lisa asked.

"I'm sure it will have to be cancelled," he said. Then Harold Cross looked directly at Lisa and continued: "This may make a change in my status, and I will probably be transferred. If you don't hear from me, you will know that I am gone."

Lisa couldn't believe her ears. "Why in the world would this cause Harold Cross to be transferred? She knew instinctively that she shouldn't ask questions, so she just said, "I'm sorry."

After Harold Cross left, the maintenance crew sergeant entered the club. "Have you heard the bad news?" he asked.

"Yes. I suppose this means we'll have to cancel the dance, but I don't know how we can do that. The hall and dance band have been hired, and all of the refreshments are ready. I suppose we could call and cancel everything. I'm sure it has been done before."

"No," he said. "We've put too much effort into this, and it's especially important for morale to do it tonight."

"I don't know about that,"Lisa said. "We'd probably get into trouble."

"Never," the sergeant answered. "There will be too many of us. We'll pick you up at 8:30."

Against her better judgement, Lisa agreed, but she was uneasy. Nevertheless, when the military truck came for her at 8:30, she meekly climbed into the back of the truck which was already crowded with GI's. The sergeant lowered the flap across the back, and warned everyone to keep silent particularly when they drove through the guard gate. "You can start talking when we get to Bury St. Edmunds," he said.

Lisa's fears subsided after she entered the dance hall. The band and many of the girls and members of the maintenance crews were already there. However, as the evening wore on, enthusiasm seemed to wane. The GI's also were thinking of the men who had died that day, and the planes that were lost, and it was difficult for them, as well as for Lisa, to get into a party mood. Lisa began to think that it had all been a mistake, and she asked the sergeant to take her back to the base. "You were right," he said. "We probably shouldn't have done this. I think I'll call the whole thing off and we'll all return to the base."

The dance ended at 11:00 P.M. and Lisa and the sergeant had left the hall to start back to the base when Lisa was surprised to see Lt. Winston in a command car waiting for her. He was frowning, and Lisa knew he was displeased with her.

"I've come to take you back to the base," he said. "It's an order."

Lisa entered Lt. Winston's command car and waited for the driver to start off before she spoke: "Why did you come for me?"she asked.

"I'm trying to keep you out of trouble," he replied.

"Am I in trouble?"

"Anyone who leaves a restricted base is in trouble. They will list the names of the enlisted men who attended the dance, and I didn't want you to be amongst them."

"And why not?"

"Because I don't want to be responsible for a new Red Cross club director and have to go through what I've had to go through with you."

"Has it been all that bad?"

Lt Winston relaxed and almost smiled when he said, "No, it hasn't been that bad, but any new girl would be lost for a while if she tried to take over from where you are now."

"What about you? Will you be in trouble for leaving the base?"

"I hope not. But you never know."

"I hope not, too. I would feel very guilty if I caused you trouble."

"We'll see."

The next day, Lisa learned that Lt. Winston was indeed in trouble. He had been restricted to quarters, and there was talk that he would be court-marshaled. This message was relayed to Lisa by the sergeant who seemed pleased that Lt. Winston would be getting his due. Lisa, however, was devastated. "It's all my fault," she said. "I'll have to go see the Colonel and tell him that I am to blame."

"I think you'd better wait a while," the sergeant said. "Maybe we'll all be court-marshaled. You, too."

Lisa had never known a time when she had been so devastated by feelings of guilt and anxiety. Most of all Lisa dreaded having to tell Andy that she and Lt. Winston, and the maintenance crew men might all be court-marshaled. But she knew she had to do it as soon as he returned from London, before anyone else told him.

It was late afternoon on Monday when Andy arrived at the club and walked into the kitchen where Lisa and Jane were preparing snacks for the evening rush. He was smiling and looked cheerful, which surprised Lisa. "Have you heard the bad news?" Lisa asked.

"Yes," Andy replied. "But it isn't all bad. All missions have been cancelled, and even if the base has been restricted, you and I can have a drink at the Officers' Club now and then, and perhaps a cup of coffee here. That's more than we've been able to do for a long time."

"I know," Lisa said, "but I have something to tell you, and I hope you won't be angry with me."

"I could never be angry with you," Andy said as he took her hand.

Andy, true to his word, was not angry, but he was immediately concerned. Quietly and gently he explained to her the importance of the base restriction. "The command probably thinks there may be a spy around who tipped off the Germans that we would raid at that time and place. We all thought the Germans may have been alerted and were waiting for our planes. Our men didn't have a chance."

Lisa felt sick. "I'm so sorry," she said, "And Lt. Winston is in trouble, too, and I'm partially to blame. I don't care if they court-martial me. That's what they should do."

"They won't court-martial you," Andy assured her, "but I don't know about Lt. Winston. It's a pretty serious matter."

Lisa was grateful that Andy was not angry. Tears came to her eyes, and she suggested that they go for a walk. She needed to tell Andy, away from prying eyes, that she loved him, and would try not to cause any more trouble. As they walked out of sight around the coal pile, Andy took her in his arms and said: "Don't worry," Lisa, "Nothing in this world can destroy my love for you. It's forever. When the restrictions are lifted, I'll come for you, and we'll drive into Bury St. Edmunds, and maybe find a little privacy where I can tell you better."

When Lisa returned to the club, Lt. Winston was there waiting for her. He had come to tell Lisa that charges had been dropped against everyone. "There were just too many involved," he said. "But we've all learned a valuable lesson. There won't be any more ignoring orders by this officer."

"Nor by this Aero Club director," Lisa said. Then with a smile she added: "But if I should, I don't want you to rescue me."

"Don't worry," he said, "I won't."

CHAPTER 18

MANAGERESS AND ACCOUNTANT

Mickey was right about the manageress and accountant being important, particularly in England. Lisa was sure that things would be much easier for her if she could have the help of a manageress and accountant. But after their arrival at the club, she soon learned that ignorance was bliss, and she understood at long last why she was always being threatened with jail or fines by one Ministry or another.

In England, you were required to make daily reports in quadruplicate for every bite of food taken out of locked storage rooms. These forms were then submitted to the Food Ministry, the Food department at Red Cross headquarters, and two were kept on file at the club. At the end of the month, all of this daily data was gathered together, and the manageress would then make a trip to the Food Ministry where she would enter into lengthy negotiations before she could obtain ration points for the next month's supply.

Besides attending to the intricacies of the food situation, the manageress was charged with hiring help. It was she who was supposed to determine whether a serving girl was under fifteen, or only said she was, or whether a cook was on first priority and therefore could not be hired by a third-priority organization. It was she who had to determine whether the labor card which all persons who were drafted by the Ministry of Labor carried with them, was in proper order. It was she who determined the hours the help should work, and saw to it that protocol was strictly observed. A cook could never wash dishes, and a serving girl could never scrub floors. Lunch hours had to be staggered to prevent cooks and serving girls from eating at the same table with scrubwomen, and the manageress and accountant must be provided with a table and dining area of their own.

The accountant, even more than the manageress was an entity unto herself, responsible only to the accounting office at Red Cross headquarters in London. She was completely outside the jurisdiction of the club director. So, when she came, it was to be presumed that Lisa would be completely free of money worries, and would never again fret about how long the butcher, the baker, and the brick-yard owner would be willing to extend credit, or whether there would be enough money from the proceeds of each day's sales to pay off the help that night, or whether the P.X. Officer would be forever willing to lend Lisa change when the till ran short.

Lisa often thought during those early days, that her trials would have been considerably less if she had had an accountant and manageress with her from the start, as Mickey had warned. But after they came, she wasn't so sure.

Mickey drove into town to meet the manageress and accountant at the depot, and drove triumphantly to the quarters where Lisa was waiting to greet them. As Mickey helped the women from the Crosley he was obviously pleased. "I told you they would come." he said to Lisa.

The manageress, Miss Handel, was a short, prim, Irish woman, who was pushing middle age and was decidedly old-maidish in both her mannerisms and appearance, and she had an annoying habit of simpering whenever there was a man around.

The accountant was a frail little Cockney girl, whose name was Ann Wilson. She spoke with such a heavy accent that it was difficult for Lisa to understand what she was saying. However, she came equipped with account books, a bank account of five hundred pounds, and a thorough understanding of her job.

The accountant, Ann Wilson, seemed quite capable, but Miss Handel seemed at a loss about how to handle her job as a manageress. She was displeased with everything from the start. A flood of tears was turned on for the first time when Lisa showed her and Ann to their rooms in the hut. Lisa had obtained a bed and a chest for each room, and Nick had cut some kindling and had laid a fire in the little stove, ready for lighting. Lisa thought they would be pleased.

But Miss Handel complained: "I can't live in a place like this. It isn't fit for a human being. Why, there isn't even a wardrobe closet to hang my clothes in. They'll all be ruined from coal soot, and we can't get more like you Americans can. We're rationed, you know."

Lisa explained limply: "I tried to obtain a wardrobe closet for you, but there are none left at the quartermaster department. Perhaps Lt. Winston will know where I can get some. I'll ask him."

Miss Handel's sobs lessened a bit and she peeped at Lisa from tear-reddened eyes above a handkerchief she held in readiness at her nose.

"I'll stay tonight," she compromised, "but if I don't get a wardrobe tomorrow, I'll go back to headquarters, and tell them I can't live in a place like this."

Miss Handel was a black-mailer, but Lisa didn't know it then. She was willing to turn Heaven and Earth if necessary the next day in order to find a wardrobe closet to keep Miss Handel from leaving. She would ask Lt. Winston to help. He could do anything.

The accountant, Ann Cox, went about her business without saying a word. She arranged her books on the table and placed her clothing in the chest. Lisa knew that whatever might happen, Ann would stay, and she was relieved.

But it was a shock when Ann informed Lisa that she would not be responsible for any money transactions or agreements Lisa had entered into before her arrival at the club. Ann would pay all bills contracted on or after the day of her arrival, but any Lisa might have incurred before that time, would be Lisa's own responsibility. Lisa had kept a record of the bills she had incurred and they were considerable, what with bricks, mortar, lumber for bookcases, paint, brushes, and turpentine to say nothing of groceries, bakery goods and coca-cola supplies. She handed the list to Ann.

"Coo," Ann said, "I would'na have know wha to do wi these."

Lisa left the two women to settle themselves in the quarters, explaining that she still had things to do at the club. Actually, Lisa needed time to ponder the change in circumstances. There would be two women in the quarters with her, and that would be a help during the lonely nights. But she was not sure she would get along well with Miss Handel, and she was concerned about the bills she could not pay. Her heavy thoughts were happily interrupted when she saw Andy riding his bike up the walk towards her. When he came alongside, he said: "I thought you might like to go for a ride down a romantic country lane to visit Amy and Fred. I think they would like to hear about the things we're planning. And it's just about tea-time."

"I can't think of anything that would please me more," Lisa said. "I'll get some doughnuts, and be right back."

It was a lovely evening as Lisa and Andy biked down the lane. The weather had warmed a bit, and Lisa was glad to be free of the tension of dealing with Miss Handel and Miss Cox. When Lisa and Andy arrived at the Majors' cottage, Amy opened the door. "It's so nice to see you," Amy greeted them, and you both look so happy."

"Indeed we are happy," Andy said. "And we've come to tell you why."

"I'll pour some tea," Amy said as Lisa handed her the bag of doughnuts. "It will be good to hear something happy. There's so much unhappiness these days."

"I could stand to hear something happy, too," Fred Major said as he placed two more cups on the table.

As soon as they were seated, Andy told them that he and Lisa were planning a wedding at the village church. There were tears of joy in Amy's eyes as she took Lisa's hand in her own. "I'm so happy for you," she said. "Please let us help with the arrangements. It will mean so much to us."

"You don't know how much your offer means to me," Lisa said as she put her hand over Amy's. "You will be my family for this occasion."

"And mine, too," Andy added.

"And you will be our children," Fred Major said.

When Lisa and Andy arrived back at the club, and were parking their bikes against the hut, Lisa said, "You know Andy, I'm beginning to feel that England is a second home to me. I feel safe and secure and loved here."

"Well, loved anyway." Andy said, "But not very safe. I know you worry about my safety, but I worry about you, too. All of England is a target for the Germans, and we can't forget that."

"Somehow I don't feel that I'm a target anymore. I feel confident that I'm going to make it, and you will make it with me."

"Keep thinking that way," Andy said. "In the meantime, let's make the most of the time I'm off missions."

The next day Lisa watched anxiously for Harold Cross to come into the club. He would not be reporting about Andy because Andy was not on a mission, but sometimes he came in just to say Hello, and to report good news if all the planes came back O.K. But this morning he did not show up, and she wondered. Could he have been the spy? If so, what would they do to him? Somehow she didn't think Harold Cross would do a thing like that.

It was Lt. Winston who soon entered the club. "It was a good day," he said. "All the planes came back."

"Thank you so much," Lisa said. "Will you be keeping me informed from now on? I don't suppose Harold Cross will be around to do it."

"No, he's not on the base anymore," Lt. Winston said. "I'll do what I can."

CHAPTER 19

DOUGHNUT DOLLIES IN THE FIELD

Lisa gradually became aware of the important role that the American Red Cross was playing in boosting the morale of the overseas soldiers. In spite of everything that could be done, time would hang heavy for restless and bored soldiers, and they needed unlimited amounts of diversion to direct their attention away from the routine, fears, frustrations, and tragedies of army life.

Bob Hope, James Cagney, Frances Langford, Betty Grable, Glenn Miller, Fred Astaire, the wonderful entertainers with the U.S.O. all contributed to making life a little easier for the men and women who were risking their lives in the war effort. The entertainment department of the Red Cross with headquarters in London, organized camp shows from a combination of English and American talent, and sent them from base to base throughout England. The entertainment department also sent a movie operator with somewhat ancient films to club directors upon request. All of this was a great help to club directors who needed variety in their entertainment programs. Show girls in particular, caused a sensation wherever they went, and Lt. Winston exerted great effort to build comfortable dressing rooms for them in back of the stage in the movie theater he had established on the base. He also acted as their official host when they came to the base, conducting them about the base. Lisa did her part too, often serving coffee and doughnuts to the cast.

The American Red Cross established clubs like the one in Bury St. Edmunds which were close to military bases where soldiers could spend a few hours on their free evenings away from army routine.

The Red Cross clubmobile girls, too, were always warmly welcomed when they came to the field to greet the fliers when they came home from their missions. The clubmobile girls were young, light-hearted, and they sang and wise-cracked with the men as they served steaming hot coffee, freshly made doughnuts, and played the latest jive records over their loudspeakers. The men showed their appreciation of the clubmobile girls by affectionately calling them their "Doughnut Dollies."

The special responsibility of helping to maintain the daily morale of the soldiers in the field fell to the aero club director and her staff. They spent many hours exclaiming over worn photographs of wives, sweethearts, and children. They tried to cheer the soldiers whose loved ones had not written. They listened sympathetically when a combat man spoke dismally of his chances of survival and his fear of dying. They also fought a constant battle to stay cheerful, even when they learned that friends they had joked and laughed with had not returned from a mission. Nevertheless, there were times when Lisa felt that she could not handle the tragedies that constantly overwhelmed her, and particularly when she could do nothing to help. One such occurrence involved a young bombardier from Texas who came into her office, sat down, and began to talk. His older brother, also a bombardier who had been stationed on a nearby base with a B-17 group had lost his life over enemy territory when he was hit by enemy fire. The young airman was concerned about his mother. "This will kill her," he said. "He was her pride and joy."

Lisa was at a loss to know what to say. How does one console a young man who was grieving over such a tragedy?

His next statement alarmed her. "You know what I'm going to do? I'm going to apply to take his place on the B-17, and I'm going to give those Krauts a dose of their own medicine."

"How would that help your mother?" Lisa asked softly. But the airman wasn't listening. He had made up his mind. The next time Lisa saw him he was in the dining hall surrounded by a group of fellow fliers. He had returned from the B-17 base for a visit with his former comrades, and was excitedly relating his experiences as a bombardier on a B-17 bomber. The next Lisa heard, he had also lost his life. Lisa thought of his mother. Two fine, courageous, wonderful young sons lost within a few months.

One by one Lisa added recreational programs to club activities. She organized ping-pong tournaments, card games, dart tournaments, bicycle picnics, bingo games, phonograph dances, foreign language classes and dancing classes.

Most recreational activities were possible, and fairly easy to accomplish, but some GI requests were not so simple. Some of the men on the base had become obsessed with the idea of forming a jazz band. They had been professional musicians in civilian life, and they yearned to blow a horn, beat a drum, or pound a piano. They followed Lisa about the club pleading with her to obtain musical instruments for them, just as if she had magic powers and could produce musical instruments out of thin air.

Finally Lisa succumbed to their pleas to the extent that she made a special trip to London headquarter's purchasing department to try to obtain the instruments they wanted. Lisa was delighted to find that Mr. Briggs, who had been the Red Cross commander during her trip to England on H.M.S. Rangitata, was the head of the Red Cross purchasing department in London.

Mr. Briggs greeted her cordially, "It's very good to see you again."

"It's good to see you, too," Lisa replied. "I wish I had known before now that you were in charge of purchasing. There are ever so many things I've been needing. The reason I came today, however, is to obtain musical instruments to start a jazz band on the base."

Mr. Briggs promised that he would do everything humanly possible to comply with Lisa's request. "But," he warned. "All musical instruments in England have been placed in the strategic material classification, and the army has frozen distribution. I understand that they've got thousands of instruments locked in warehouses, and no-one can get them out. However, I'll try to buy some for you on the English market."

Lisa returned to the base confident that Mr. Briggs would manage to fulfill her request, and he did. Shortly thereafter, a truck from the Ministry of Works drove into the courtyard and unloaded a large packing box labeled: "Hilly Billy Band."

The Hilly Billy Band consisted of two accordions, two banjos, two ukeleles, and a fiddle, which proved to be popular with many amateur musicians who dropped into the club and played for numerous song-fests. It was not, however, what the professional musicians had envisioned, and they would have none of it.

As always when Lisa had an impossible problem that needed solving, she turned to Lt. Winston. He and his undercover scroungers who toured the countryside in search of this and that, uncovered an English civilian band that was disorganizing, and Lt. Winston bought all of their instruments with a loan he floated from the Officers' Club. With his usual ingenuity, he also contacted a replacement depot, and obtained permission to have professional musicians assigned to the base.

Within a few days the musicians were practicing on the theater stage, and in a few weeks their "Skyliner's Band" was ready to play for the dance at the official opening of Lisa's club, and to book other engagements at other bases all over the Kingdom.

However, Lt. Winston soon discovered that running competition to Harry James was not a simple matter. All of the musicians were on full-time army duty and some were combat men. Often a crisis occurred when the band was scheduled to play for an important function, and at the same time some of the musicians were ordered to fly a bombing mission over Germany. Commanding officers understandably took a dim view of excusing combat men to play in a dance band. Nevertheless, the Skyliner's Band became one of the best GI bands in England, and soon after its first appearance at Lisa's official club opening, it was receiving requests from headquarters groups and officers' clubs as well as from Red Cross organizations. The Skyliner's Band played for several Saturday evening bookings at the famed Covent Gardens dance hall in London, and was offered a steady booking there. Many times it broadcast on radio programs to the United States. Certainly it played a part in keeping up the morale of American soldiers in England.

And for Lisa and Andy the Skyliner's Band was a Godsend. Lisa depended upon it to play for GI dances in the club, and she and Andy spent many pleasant hours dancing in the Officers' Club and in other Clubs on near-by bases, where it was in great demand.

CHAPTER 20

ENTER ... EXIT ... MISS MAPLES

Lt. Winston was creating miracles at the club. With his GI crew of volunteer carpenters, brick-layers, painters, and decorators, the fireplaces were a reality and Lisa thought as lovely as any she had ever seen in the States. The walls in all of the buildings had been painted in various pastel colors, and book shelves were being built for the library. The army had taken over one building and was busily remodeling it into the likeness of an English pub. They were painting the walls a bright pink, and a sign "Pink Pub" had already been installed across the door, and the walls had been decorated with Petty Girl posters and photographs of Betty Grable and other glamorous stars. Soon the army would start serving beer there during the evening hours.

Lisa, however, was still having difficulties with her staff.

Lisa discovered that there was such a thing as a kitchen supervisor. Her name was Miss Maples and she arrived at the club unannounced. Lisa soon learned that a kitchen supervisor was supposed to hire the staff, negotiate with the Ministry of Food for ration points, and instruct the staff in its duties.

Miss Maples, therefore, was not prepared to find a club already in operation, and a kitchen staff working for lo' these last two months. Miss Maples was frightfully frustrated!

Lisa was at lunch at the officers' mess hall when Miss Maples arrived. Nick came running to get her.

"Somebody important!" he said, his eyes round with urgency, "and she's mad, awful mad. You better come quick!"

"All right, Nick," Lisa agreed. "I'll have my coffee at the club. Do you have any idea who she is?"

Nick shook his head. "No, I don't know. But she comes from headquarters."

On the way back to the club, Lisa tried to think who at headquarters might have new cause to be angry with her. When she saw Miss Maples she was still puzzled, because Lisa had never seen her before. Middle-aged, frouzy headed, and built like a jeep, Miss Maples was standing in the middle of the kitchen with her hands on her hips and her face like a thundercloud.

Miss Maples did not return Lisa's greeting. Instead, she glared at Lisa and snapped: "What do you think you are doing here?"

Her question stumped Lisa. She wasn't sure what she was doing herself, but she couldn't tell Miss Maples that. "I'm the club director," Lisa replied tentatively, hoping her answer would clarify the situation.

It didn't. Miss Maples appeared not even to have heard, as she continued: "Who gave you authority to open this club without my knowledge?"

At this point Lisa was becoming irritated. "I could hardly have told you when I don't even know who you are."

Miss Maples pressed her hands against her hips more firmly and squinted her eyes to a fine slit before she answered: "I am the kitchen supervisor." She spoke as if she were announcing herself as the Queen of England.

"Oh, yes," Lisa answered, relieved that she had placed her as a more or less inconsequential executive, instead of the successor to the Commissioner. "My field director mentioned something about a kitchen supervisor several months ago. I've been expecting you all this time, but now everything seems to be coming along nicely. I don't suppose there will be much for you to do."

"Not much for me to do!" Miss Maples snorted. "We shall see about that. It is my responsibility to set up this kitchen, and that is what I intend to do."

"But it's all set up," Lisa explained.

"We shall see about that. We shall see," Miss Maples repeated. "And what have you done about your ration points?"

Lisa answered as civilly as she could. "I went down to the Food Ministry, and they very kindly filled out the proper forms, and gave me my ration books."

"And what makes you think that you are capable of driving a hard bargain with them?"

"I didn't try to drive a hard bargain. I just asked for my fair share, and that, I'm sure is what I got. Now if you've no other business, will you please excuse me?"

"Indeed I will," Miss Maples spewed. "But we're not finished with this yet," and leaving Lisa hot and angry behind her, she stalked out of the kitchen.

Soon Lisa heard Miss Maples' car backing out of the courtyard as she left for town. But Miss Maples meant what she said. Lisa wasn't finished with her yet...not nearly.

The next morning it became acutely and painfully apparent to Lisa that Miss Maples intended to set up a kitchen in the club, and had decided that in order to do it, she first had to demolish the one that was already there. Her first step towards this goal was to stop at the Food Ministry in Bury St. Edmunds where she cancelled all of Lisa's food ration points, taking the ration books to London headquarters with her.

Lisa learned what Miss Maples had done when the bakery man came to deliver some cakes the next morning. "I'm sorry this must be my last delivery," he said. "I hope you were not dissatisfied."

"What do you mean, your last delivery?" Lisa asked. "I don't want you to stop deliveries."

"I can't make cakes without ration points," he replied, "and I have been informed by the Ministry of Food that you have cancelled your ration points to me."

"Miss Maples," Lisa said to herself. "She's the rat in the food bin."

Lisa reached for the phone, and in a few moments was connected with the Ministry of Food office.

A woman answered Lisa's query: "A representative of the American Red Cross was in yesterday afternoon. She cancelled all of your food ration books, and told us she would get in touch with us later to have new ones issued."

"Thank you," Lisa said, and hung up. Mild-tempered Lisa was angry, so angry in fact, that she felt like murdering someone... Miss Maples, to be exact. But she cooled down enough to persuade the baker to continue delivering cakes and pastries until she could get the situation straightened out.

Lisa considered the possibility of catching the next train to London to take care of Miss Maples personally, but decided against such rash action, mainly because she didn't have time to go to London. She called Mr. Allen, head of the field service in London, instead.

Lisa told Mr. Allen about the cancellation of her ration books, and explained that if they were not sent back at once, there would be no food on the counters at the club, the kitchen staff would have nothing to do to earn their salaries, and the men at the base would be complaining about the inefficiency of the American Red Cross and demanding that the NAAFI be returned.

"Just a moment," Mr. Allen interrupted her. "I'll find out what Miss Maples has done with your ration books."

Mr. Allen came back on the line, and informed Lisa that Miss Maples had gone out of town and her secretary said she was not expected back for a week. "Miss Maples has left your books locked in her desk," he said. "There's nothing that can be done until she returns."

"You can break her desk open with an axe," Lisa said with unnatural firmness. "I don't care what you have to do, but I must have those books back within a day or two."

After she hung up the phone, Lisa was appalled when she realized that she had been rude to her boss. However, in a few days the ration books arrived by mail without comment from Mr. Allen.

Yet Lisa had not seen the last of Miss Maples. Lisa was ill in bed with a high fever when Miss Maples arrived again. The base medical officer had ordered Lisa to stay in bed until he released her, and the Commanding Officer of the group, who maintained a fatherly concern for everyone, had heard of Lisa's illness and had come to see how she was. He had barely seated himself on the chair by the bed, when there was a knock at the door, and one of the cleaning women came into the room sobbing. "I'm giving notice," she said. "I'm a respectable housewife, and I thought I could help in the war effort by working in a Yank canteen, but I won't be treated like a dog!"

The woman was one of Lisa's most conscientious cleaning women, and Lisa didn't want to lose her. "Don't quit," Lisa pleaded. "Miss Maples will leave tomorrow and everything will be all right again." Pacified, the cleaning woman nodded agreement and left the room.

The door had barely closed behind the cleaning woman when it flew open again, and in came Miss Handel, her handkerchief at her nose, and tears flooding from red-rimmed eyes. "I'm leaving," she wailed. "No one has ever treated me like this, and I won't put up with it."

Patiently, Lisa set out to mollify Miss Handel. Finally the sobs subsided, and Miss Handel minced her way to the door, not so unstrung that she neglected to simper at the Colonel as she passed by him.

The Colonel, who had been an amazed onlooker to both of the tearful demonstrations turned to Lisa when she had gone. "Does this sort of thing go on all of the time over here?"he asked.

"No," Lisa replied. "Only when that woman comes here. She's trying to destroy the club, and I don't know why. Maybe she's a Jerry sympathizer or something, but if I don't get out of this bed, and get over there she will have purged the whole staff before..."

Lisa was interrupted by Mickey who charged into the room in such distress that he didn't even notice that the C.O. was there. He shook a finger in Lisa's face, and his unruly hair seemed to be fairly standing on end as he shouted at her. "You've got to get up, and get this club in shape. Everything's wrong. Everything."

"I can't get out of bed until the Medical Officer says I can," Lisa said. And with more than a little malice, she added: "Miss Maples is your baby. You do as you like with her."

"If I tell her to leave," Mickey bargained, recognizing defeat, "will you get tough with the help?"

Lisa started to reply, but was interrupted by the Colonel who spoke slowly, deliberately. Looking directly at Mickey, he said: "You tell that woman to get off this base at once, or I'll have her escorted off by the Military Police."

"Yes, Sir." Mickey said.

When Mickey had gone, Lisa laughed and the Colonel did, too, Lisa was laughing because the Colonel had solved so many distressing problems with just one short sentence. She felt wonderful.

"Is there such a thing as psychosomatic fever?" she asked the Colonel.

"I don't know," the Colonel replied, "but if there is, you have every reason to contract it."

CHAPTER 21

MUD, DIRECTIVES, RATS, SPIES, EARWIGS AND WEDDING PLANS

The rainy season in England seemed to operate on a full-time basis from January to June when it loafed on a half-time schedule until the next January. Ordinarily Lisa liked the pitter-patter of rain on the roof, but there can be too much of anything, and there was too much rain in England, even though the tin roofs of the Nissen huts were particularly adaptable to pitter-patter.

The worst effect of the rain was the mud it caused. At the base it remained ankle-high, and was of an adhesive quality that clung to GI boots like glue until it dried out in the warmth of the club. Then it dropped to the floor where it was trampled by thousands of heavy boots into a paste-like covering inches thick.

Nick was seldom seen without a broom or mop, waging a desperate battle against the mud that was carried in faster than he could mop it up.

Running a close second to the mud as an irritant, were the rats. At least several hundred families of them had established themselves between the tin walls of the club where they set up housekeeping, organized governments, and waged nightly wars. Often, Lisa would be startled right out of her chair by the piercing death wail of a defeated rat. And Miss Handel, who would pretend to faint at the sight of a mouse, would screech at Lisa: "Rats!" Why don't you do something about those rats?"

Then Miss Handel added an insult and a warning: "I must say, Americans have an odd idea of sanitation. If the rats don't leave, I shall."

There were times when Lisa thought the rats were preferable to Miss Handel and perhaps she should keep them.

Miss Handel may have been entitled to more sympathy than Lisa was inclined to give her, because aside from the normal irritations which afflicted everyone who lived on the base, Miss Handel was also plagued by queer creatures called earwigs. The medical officer seemed a bit vague about how they could be eradicated, but to Miss Handel at least, they were very real. They crawled into her ears at night, she said, and were about to drive her to distraction. Indeed, the way she went about shaking her head, grimacing, and mumbling to herself, it was possible to believe that she had already been driven.

Then, as if Miss Handel hadn't enough trouble, she brought more on herself by writing a letter to her family in Ireland in which she reported that the Americans and rats, being brothers under the skin, lived together and liked it. The letter was picked up by British Intelligence, which took a dim view of insults to the American rescue forces, and Miss Handel almost lost her job.

British Intelligence and American G2 forces were very important to the war effort. Lisa remembered that Andy had told her that a spy had informed the Germans of an impending American raid which caused the loss of all American planes on the mission. The spy danger was also brought home to Lisa when she heard a rumor that an inconspicuous little Hungarian farmer who often came to the club selling frying chickens, was picked up as a spy by British Intelligence, and was convicted and executed.

Then there was the day when a German Messerschmitt fighter landed on the base. Nick came running into Lisa's office to tell her. He was excited and alarmed, but Lisa was curious. "You're kidding," she said, "I'm going to see."

"I wouldn't if I were you," Nick warned.

But Lisa was already on the way to the quarters where she mounted her bike and pedalled toward the landing field. Sure enough, a German fighter plane was there and handsome young crew men were climbing out with their hands in the air. The Military Police immediately took them into custody. It was, Lisa learned later, a surrender by German fliers who had become disillusioned with the German war.

Then there were the directives which came to Mickey from headquarters that he was forever producing at the most inopportune times. One such was a gem of a directive that ordered club directors to have the entire staff inoculated for small pox, typhus, tetanus, and diphtheria and to have a chest X-ray for tuberculosis and a Schick test for venereal disease, before they could be hired!

"You see," Mickey accused. "You've done it all wrong. Now you've got to fire everybody."

"That's a bit drastic," Lisa said. "Maybe they all won't have communicable diseases. Maybe I can salvage a scrub woman or two."

But Mickey was serious about directives. "It says here that you've got to fire them because you shouldn't have hired them in the first place unless they'd had the shots and the tests."

When Lisa realized that Mickey was serious about firing the staff, she became alarmed. "Let's not jump off the deep end because of this directive," she argued. "If we fire everybody, we'll have to close the club. It may be weeks before we can open it again because help is hard to find this far out in the country. Beside, we'll have to wait six weeks until they complete the shots, even if they agree to have them. I think I should talk to the staff first, and maybe I can persuade them to let me take them in to the hospital at Bury St. Edmunds for the shots, and keep them working in the meantime."

"All right," Mickey agreed. "But if they don't get the shots, out they go."

"I'll do my best to see that they do it."

But the staff let Lisa down. They refused to have the shots. In desperation Lisa pledged them all to secrecy, and they agreed that Lisa would tell Mickey that they were all in the process of taking the shots. Fortunately, Lisa's honor and integrity were not brought into question, because several weeks later, Mickey received a directive from headquarters that the order for immunization shots had been rescinded. Someone at headquarters had decided that they were not necessary after all.

In spite of trials and problems with her job, Lisa was happy. Andy was seeing her every afternoon. Sometimes they drove into town for lunch or cocktails at the Angel Hotel; sometimes to the American Red Cross Club where they visited with Tom Anderson and his staff, and sometimes they rode their bikes along the village lanes and stopped in for tea with Amy and Fred Major. It was a wonderful and romantic time for Lisa, and day by day she was falling more in love with the handsome and loving pilot who was her fiance. And they were making plans. Andy had applied for a wedding license, had made arrangements for the church and had asked the base chaplain to perform the ceremony. Fred and Amy Major had assumed the responsibility of decorating the church with flower displays from local gardeners. Andy had suggested that he and Lisa take two days off in London to buy wedding rings, a wedding gown for Lisa, and plan a happy time together away from army life.

Then the inevitable happened. One evening after a bike ride Andy said, "I can't see you after the club closes this evening. I'm to be in early tonight.

The plane is ready and so is the crew and Jim Jackson will be my bombardier again. So we're ready to fly."

Lisa knew only too well what that meant. He would be flying missions in the mornings again, and Lisa would be anxiously awaiting his return.

In spite of the setbacks and disappointments, Lisa was pleased with the progress she was making at the Club. Miss Handel and Miss Cox were conscientiously doing their jobs. The club was clean, scrubbed with sudsy water until it fairly glistened. The great stoves were re-blackened daily, and a new white chalk line was painted across the base as proof that the job had been done. Gradually, the rooms were painted in bright shiny new colors. The great brick fireplaces were dispensing a glowing warmth over the GIs who lounged in front of them. Many GI's settled themselves in deep chairs to read one of the five thousand volumes, donated by the American people through the Victory Book campaign, which lined the walls of the library.

In the Snack Bar, English serving girls looked crisp and neat in their starched uniforms, and being young (under fifteen), they blushed and giggled when the GIs teased them as they served sandwiches, salads, hamburgers, cakes, sweet buns, Coca-Cola, tea, and coffee to the hundreds of GIs who lined up a block long before opening time each evening.

Army officers came to inspect the club and complimented Lisa and her staff on its attractiveness and sanitation. Sometimes they chided the GIs for throwing cigarette butts on the floor of "this beautiful club." The GIs picked up the offending butts, but showed resentment as they did so, because it was their club, and no officer had the right to tell them what to do in it. It was the enlisted man's castle, a refuge away from army routine and army discipline. It was a place where they could read in comfort, write letters home, or just sit and stare at the coals in the fireplace while listening to music from the radio-phonograph. And it was a place where they could invite their girl friends on special nights for parties and dancing, and a snack in the Snack Bar or a glass of beer in the army-operated Pink Pub.

The Red Cross was not really a part of the army, and whatever military privileges were accorded, had to be arranged by special negotiations between American Red Cross headquarters and Army headquarters in Washington D.C.

By special arrangement, therefore, Red Cross personnel received army transportation, P.X. rations, army mess privileges, hospital care, and official A.G.O. cards designating rank as "Assimilated Captain."

For the rest, Red Cross personnel were on their own. All of the staff at the club was English, either volunteers who came whenever they could to help out, or workers hired on the English labor market, and paid from American Red Cross funds. Even Nick, over Lisa's vehement protests, was called back to his own company, and returned to work on the garbage detail.

All of the food that was served at the Snack Bar counter was purchased from the pitifully frugal British stores. The club directors and the clubmobile girls received their doughnut mixture and lard by direct Red Cross shipment from the United States. All furniture and equipment was ordered by the American Red Cross, and was supplied by the English Ministry of Works.

The Red Cross was free to formulate its own policies for the good of all of the men in uniform, without regard for rank. This policy relieved the Red Cross from entering into army politics, army jealousies, and army squabbles. It also left the Red Cross field directors free to negotiate with army brass on behalf of the enlisted men. This was one of the most important Red Cross functions, even though it may have been unpopular with some army officers who considered it meddling.

The Red Cross field service was a most remarkable organization. The field director, in contact with the soldier on the field, was an almost direct link between the soldier and his family in the States. In Red Cross chapters in every community and village throughout the United States, thousands of volunteers waited to receive messages from field directors. The American Red Cross volunteers in the United States visited wives with new born babies, stood by when relatives were ill or in need, comforted families whose sons were lost to combat, loaned money in emergencies, and otherwise took the soldier's place in the family when he could not be there.

Red Cross field directors worked with the soldiers at the war fronts. Mickey, though often at odds with Lisa about club matters, was a good field director. He was compassionate, interested, and spent much time working out problems for distressed soldiers.

CHAPTER 22

A JOB WELL DONE

It was the custom for Red Cross Aero Club directors to publicize their accomplishments throughout the Red Cross hierarchy and to the soldiers they served, by staging an official opening celebration when the club was completed. Each club director planned the festivities for that big day, and invited those executives at London headquarters who were directly concerned with aero club operations, and others who might be interested indirectly. It was the aero club director's chance to show what she had accomplished, and it was also a good reason for a big party for the soldiers who had helped in the effort.

Lisa planned an afternoon tea party to be held in the library, to which she invited the executives in the field service at London headquarters, as well as people like Mrs. Sloane Colt representing the Red Cross Commissioner, Mr. McHenry, who was head of the Red Cross publicity department, military brass from the Bomb Group, and the Clerk of the Works, Mr. Randall, and his boss in Cambridge, Mr. Leaven. All accepted the invitation.

For the soldiers, Lisa planned an evening dance, with several hundred English girls as guests, free snacks, Coca-Cola and coffee, and music by the Skyliner's Band.

The planning and execution of such a celebration involved many details. First Lisa located the girls who were to be invited, and arranged for transportation to bring them from their quarters to the base, and take them home again. Obviously the thing to do was to invite service girls exclusively, and issue special invitations to girls who were not in the service, but were friends of soldiers at the field.

The transportation officer at the base cooperated by authorizing a command car and a driver for Lisa for a day to contact girls within a twenty mile radius of the base.

Driving about to various service camps in search of girls was a rare opportunity for Lisa to learn at first-hand what a great contribution the English women were making towards the effort to win the war.

Lisa and the driver traveled many miles that day, and visited numerous land army camps where young English girls tilled the fields, tended live-stock, and cut and milled lumber at logging mills. The girls were dressed in khaki shirts and shorts and they looked healthy and tanned from working outdoors.

Lisa also visited barracks where there were girls who manned anti-aircraft guns and shot down Jerry planes. She learned that Winston Churchill's own daughter, Mary, was a member of this service, and was manning an anti-aircraft gun in London. She located ambulance and lorry drivers, and visited British air fields where she extended invitations to girls from the WAAF (Women's Auxiliary Air Force).

At each of the camps Lisa contacted the woman officer in command, left invitations with her, and later contacted her by telephone to make arrangements for transportation. Motor pool drivers were then assigned to collect specific groups of girls and each driver was charged with the responsibility for the girls in his group.

English civilians who had heard about the club offered to help make the opening day a success. The owner of a nearby estate sent word that he would like to furnish flowers from his extensive gardens "to cheer the Yank canteen." The day before the official opening of the club, the Motor Pool sent a driver to pick up Lisa and they drove the few miles to the estate which was a veritable fairyland of beautiful blooms. There must have been thousands of rhododendron bushes, azaleas, and other flowering shrubs that almost covered the walks with an extravagance of color and perfume, and hung in massive profusion over rustic benches which were tucked into nooks along the walkways. It was easy to imagine that once Lords and Ladies, and maybe even Princes and Princesses walked through these gardens.

Only an elderly caretaker was left there to tend the grounds as best he could. Early in the war a Jerry bomb had destroyed the huge mansion house, and the Lord and his Lady who lived there, had moved away. The house was a ruin...a great mass of rubble in the center of the estate. The caretaker told us how it happened: "The Lord and Lady and all of the servants were asleep in outside rooms, and not one of them received so much as a scratch because the bomb fell through the center. It was a miracle, indeed."

The caretaker carried a long pole with a blade attached, with which he cut the loveliest blooms from the very tops of the trees. He generously loaded the jeep high with the beautiful flowers.

Back at the base, Lisa called Lt. Winston to ask if he knew of anyone on the base who could arrange the flowers. Indeed he did. Corporal Gregus, a former florist doing duty as a cook in the GI mess, came to exclaim happily over what he called the "opportunity of a florist's life."

Another English civilian who offered an unexpected gift was an antique dealer in Bury St. Edmunds who telephoned Lisa to tell her that he would like to lend some pictures to decorate the walls of the Yank canteen. Lisa thought perhaps he had some inexpensive copies he thought might be cheerful in a canteen, but when she entered his shop to accept his offer, he said: "Choose any you like. You're welcome to any or all of them."

Lisa was surprised by his generosity, but he explained: "I have a son with the Eighth Army in Africa. If I can help in any way, I am glad to do so."

Lisa thought the club was beautiful, beyond any expectations she may have had. Corporal Gregus had decorated every room with floral designs that she had never seen equaled anyplace. Everything was spotlessly clean, and the fireplaces added their touch of warmth and good cheer.

Everything was in order and proceeding nicely. The kitchen staff had been saving rations for weeks, and had spent the entire preceding day baking pastries, cakes, and making sandwiches. On celebration day they were planning to make doughnuts in the fish-fryer. The porter set a fire under the big grease vat, and the whole thing exploded into flames. Someone shrieked, "Fire," and Lisa rushed into the kitchen where the staff was already running about in the smoke, rescuing trays of sandwiches and cakes. Lisa ran back to the office and phoned the fire department. In a few minutes the fire brigade rushed in, in a shower of chemical spray.

When the fire had been extinguished, and the smoke had drifted out the windows, Lisa went in to survey the damage. All of the food, except the trays the staff had rescued was ruined by chemical spray. It would have been a complete disaster for Lisa's big party had it not been for the fast cooperation of the Doughnut Dollies of the Clubmobile staff, who used their own rations, and set to work immediately making doughnuts for the party.

The evening dance was festive, noisy, and apparently a huge success. The club was crowded with young men and young women in uniform. The

Skyliner's Band surprised everyone because it was so much better than anyone expected. No one had heard any band that sounded better, at least not in England. Everyone was having a wonderful time.

Lindsy McHenry, chief of the publicity department at Red Cross headquarters, came to the dance that evening. Mr. McHenry was enthusiastic about the club and wrote a number of stories about the party. Releases were sent to papers throughout the United States, and to Stars and Stripes Magazine. He also made a special radio broadcast to United States stations applauding the club and the party.

Lisa was pleased with all the compliments she received, but she thought Lt. Winston should have received more credit than he did. The reason he did not, of course, was that the club was an enlisted men's club, and officers were not supposed to be a part of it.

The compliment that Lisa would treasure throughout her life came from Mr. Leaven, head of the British Air Ministry in Cambridge who said: "I want you to know that I think the club is beautiful. I thought you might be pleased to know that hereafter I plan to have all Air Ministry recreation buildings designed with fireplaces and decorated in colors as you've done here."

"That is the nicest compliment I've ever had,"Lisa said, "and I want to thank you again for not sending me to jail for breaking regulations, and I'm happy to be your friend."

"Right-O," Mr. Leaven answered.

When it was all over, and the last girl had been put on her truck and sent back to her base, Lisa sat in the library with Lt. Winston, Mr. McHenry, Mrs. Colt, and Elsa, who had come down from her base to help. Shortly there was a knock on the door, and Captain Andy Thompson came in to join the group.

Lisa noticed at once the shiny new Captain's bars on his shoulders and exclaimed in delight. "You've earned this honor a thousand times over."

It was a happy day for Lisa, and she wanted to share her joy. "Captain Andy," she said, "Why don't you tell these good friends about our plans?"

"Nothing could give me more pleasure," he said as he put his arm around Lisa. "Lisa and I are planning to be married as soon as possible."

Lisa noted that no one was surprised. Everyone seemed to have known all along that Andy and Lisa would marry. Elsa put it into words. "Well, it's about time."

There were well wishes all around, hand shaking and hugging, and Lisa was in Seventh Heaven.

CHAPTER 23

PLANNING A WEDDING

It was the morning after the big celebration and Lisa was asleep until mid-morning. When she awoke, she found that all guests had left, and she was distressed that she had not been there to thank them for coming, and to bid them farewell. When she entered the club, she found Lt. Winston in the kitchen drinking a cup of coffee. "They all told me to tell you good-bye," he said. "Mrs. Colt said she knew you were exhausted, and asked us not to wake you. How about a cup of coffee?"

"Thank you," Lisa said, "I can hardly believe it's over, and I think we did good."

"Yes, we did" Lt. Winston agreed. "They all said it is the best aero club in England."

"I must give credit to you," Lt. Winston. "Without your direction and help I couldn't have come even close."

"Let's say we worked well together," Lt. Winston said, "and by the way, after today you are to address me as Captain Winston."

"That's wonderful," Lisa exclaimed. "It is a promotion that is certainly deserved. Do I have to salute now?"

"Of course."

After the club closed that evening Andy knocked on the door, and Lisa noted at once the stress on his face. He had been on another troublesome mission. Lisa poured a cup of coffee, and suggested that they retire to the comfort of the library where a fire was still burning in the fireplace. "You look like you need some comfort, " she said.

"All of us do," he said. "It's getting rougher by the day out there. But I didn't come over here to complain. I came to make plans for a wonderful time I'm looking forward to. I've been given permission to take Tuesday, Wednesday, and Thursday off this week for a trip to London with a dark-haired beauty, who is an American Red Cross worker and my fiancee."

Lisa laughed. "Well, that's quite a speech. I accept your invitation. Of course, I must get permission from Mickey to go with you. He wouldn't dare say no. Would he?"

"No," Andy said. "He wouldn't dare."

Lisa was surprised when Andy told her about the plans he had made: "I've received permission to marry from the Colonel and from the General at headquarters, and from the Bishop of the Church of England. They all think we're doing the right thing."

"How in the world did you do all of that in such a short time?"

"That's not all. I've made arrangements for the church, music, and Chaplain Fenley to perform the ceremony. And last, but not least, a three day honeymoon trip to Felixstowe on the English Channel."

"Felixstowe? I've never heard of it. Is it romantic?"

"I hope so. But if it isn't, I think we will do all right with romance."

"Well, I haven't been exactly idle. I've asked Elsa to be my Maid of Honor. And I've received a letter from Mr. Allen. He said I didn't have to ask his permission, but he sends his best wishes. And I would like Fred Major to give me away, if he agrees."

"He will agree, I'm sure."

Andy arose from his chair, walked over to Lisa, and pulled her from the chair into his arms. "Do you suppose we can find time to do a little love making?"

"My head is swimming already," Lisa answered.

Tuesday morning Andy came for Lisa, and Mickey drove them to the railroad station in Bury St. Edmunds where they boarded the train for London. It was the beginning of three of the most wonderful days Lisa had ever spent in her life. It was the first time she and Andy had been together, away from the demands of the American Red Cross, and the United States Air Force. For three days they were free to do as they liked. They forgot the war and the air force and the Red Cross, and acted like civilians again. Lisa bought a satin wedding gown and frivolous hat with a finger-length veil at Selfridges bridal salon. And after a frantic, town-wide search, she also bought a pair of white Paris-imported high-heeled slippers which cost fifteen pounds...sixty dollars!

Together Lisa and Andy bought matching wedding rings at a jewelry store on Bond Street. By that time it was nearing the dinner hour and they stopped at a wayside pub where Andy ordered gin and bitters for two. They sat in a corner where they thought they would be inconspicuous and no-one would notice that they were two Americans in love. When the waiter brought the drinks, Andy and Lisa sentimentally clicked glasses and toasted "to us", and Andy leaned over and kissed her. When they looked up, the other patrons in the pub were raising their glasses and smiling at Lisa and Andy. In return, Lisa and Andy raised their glasses and toasted "to you." It was a great moment for Lisa and Andy and for British - American relations.

Lisa learned more about Andy that night than she had ever known before. She learned that he was an exceptionally responsible and considerate man. When they returned to Lisa's hotel room, Andy held Lisa in his arms and spoke quietly to her. "I would very much like to share a room and a bed with you tonight," he said. "You don't know how much I would like to. But I've been thinking. I know the risks in my job, and they're high, and I would not want to leave an unwed pregnant mother, and an illegitimate child. And, I want our wedding night to be as perfect as we can make it."

There were tears in Lisa's eyes as she replied. "Thank you, Andy. I understand."

The wedding on the following Saturday was a simple but lovely ceremony. The church was a beautiful little church with ancient stained-glass windows. Corporal Gregus had decorated the altar with flowers, and had designed Lisa's bouquet of white carnations, and Elsa's bouquet of red carnations. Fred Major walked with Lisa down the aisle to join the wedding group. Elsa was wearing the blue taffeta formal Lisa had purchased in the Bury St. Edmunds dress shop, "Because," she said. "I don't think my black sequin job would be appropriate." Lisa agreed.

Andy, in dress uniform, was attended by his bombardier, Lt. Jackson.

The little church was packed with members of the aero club staff, and airmen from the base.

The simple double-ring ceremony was performed by Captain Fenley, chaplain of the bomb group. After the ceremony, Lisa and Andy added their names in the bridal book after the names of couples who had been married there for over six hundred years.

Lisa took Andy's arm and they walked down the aisle and out the door just in time to duck as a squadron of B-26 bombers roared over their heads in a congratulatory buzz.

After the wedding, Lisa and Andy boarded the train for Felixstowe, looking forward to a wonderful three days in a romantic seaside resort hotel. If Lisa and Andy had not been so irretrievably, madly in love, they might have been disappointed with the honeymoon site they had chosen.

The lovely beaches were laced with six foot high rolls of barbed wire intended to delay an invasion force. Lisa and Andy strolled hand-in-hand along the edge of the sand, listening to the unromantic sound of distant gunfire from the Continent. But Lisa was not aware of anything except her own good fortune. She truly believed that she was the most blessed young woman in the world to have married a man like Andy. Lisa had given herself...heart, mind, body and soul to the one man on earth for her.

CHAPTER 24

A NEW LIFE

When Andy and Lisa returned to the base, they were shocked to learn that their lives had been turned up-side-down. They had planned to rent a room at the Angel Hotel where they hoped they could find time to be alone once in a while, but that was not to be.

The American Red Cross supervisor for the field service came that day to inform Lisa that she was to be transferred to London immediately. There she would report to headquarters and wait for further orders.

But that was not the only shock Lisa received that day. Andy came to tell her that the entire bomb group had orders to move to another base nearer the channel.

All of Lisa and Andy's well laid plans had been demolished in one day.

It was with a heavy heart the following day that Lisa packed her suitcase and foot-locker and said good-bye to the staff and to Mickey and to Lt. Winston who had come over to bid her farewell.

Andy had been given permission to drive her to the railroad station to board the train to London, and when he drove up to the quarters, Lisa noted the sadness that enveloped him. "It doesn't seem right," he said. "We had everything going for us, and now I don't know. I'll try to get to London whenever I can, and maybe you can find time from whatever you will be doing to meet me in the little town of Braintree. We'll be stationed near there."

Lisa was crying. "I'll come as often as I can," she promised. "And Andy, will you say good-bye to the Majors for me? I will miss them."

"Of course I will," he said, "And Lisa, don't be so sad. One good thing, we won't be doing missions until after we're settled at the new base, and that will be a while. I'll have more time."

"I hadn't thought of that. It will be a help, I'm sure."

But it was with a heavy heart that Lisa kissed Andy farewell and boarded the train for London.

When Lisa reached London and had checked into the Mount Royal Hotel, she caught a taxi to the American Red Cross headquarters where she reported to Mr. Allen, who informed her that she had been transferred to the publicity department under the direction of Mr. McHenry. Lisa was pleased. "At least I'll be doing something I know something about," she said.

"From all reports, you did fine as an aero club director," Mr. Allen said.

"I'm not sure about that, but I thank you anyway for the compliment."

Actually Lisa had thought for some time that she was not cut out to be a Red Cross Aero Club director, and so she happily began the most delightful experience in her Red Cross career.

Lisa was assigned to work with an "internationalist" by the name of Harry Abbott. Harry looked more like a re-tread from the Hobo News than a Red Cross publicity reporter. He was shabbily dressed, and was missing a startling number of teeth. He was perhaps in late middle- age, but in spirit he was young forever. He was gallant, and kind, and he was an alcoholic, and Lisa liked him very much.

At the time, Harry was a British subject, and was on the English civilian staff payroll. This was a sore point with Harry because English civilians made less money than those who were on the American payroll, and Harry certainly needed more money. Harry was born in America and he thought he should have some consideration because he had once been an American. He had also been a Canadian citizen before he became a British citizen. Before the war he had lived for many years in Paris, and was in the process of becoming a French citizen when the war forced him to return to England.

Obviously, citizenship meant little to Harry, but his heart, for the moment at least, belonged to France. "Wonderful, wonderful Paris," he'd say nostalgically, "where you can drink all night, sleep all day, and where sterling income lasts forever."

Harry never had enough money to make ends meet, so he didn't try. He just spent most of his salary on liquor, ate wherever he could find free food, and whenever his rent came due, he moved to new "digs."

Harry thought that because he looked so shabby, the Red Cross should fit him out with a uniform. Lisa thought so too, because his job required that he interview celebrities and many important people in the army and allied services, who must have been quite startled at his appearance.

Nevertheless, Harry was a professional, and Lisa felt fortunate to be working with him. He wrote with imagination and ease. He could sit down at the typewriter, and within an hour produce at least ten publishable stories, all exciting and interesting, and all including a generous plug for the American Red Cross.

Harry seemed pleased that Lisa was to work with him. He had already made out a list of all of the American Red Cross clubs in London. "Choose the ones you want to cover," he said. "I'll take what's left."

There were fifteen Red Cross Clubs in Central London at that time. Seven were strictly for enlisted men, four were for officers and one at 10 Charles St. was for women officers, nurses, and Red Cross women. Several were for both officers and enlisted men, and one of the officers' clubs had been turned over to black enlisted men, who at that time served in segregated units.

The Red Cross clubs which were scattered about London served good, and sometimes excellent food, maintained dormitories, provided constant and varied recreational activities, and offered help, advice and consolation to thousands of homesick soldiers who came to London on leave.

The huge Rainbow Club which opened in December, 1942 in Piccadilly could host 2,000 men, and employed a staff of over 400 and was the largest club in England. The Rainbow Club functioned as a distribution center, funneling the men to the other clubs. Adele Astair, sister and dancing partner of Fred Astaire, worked in an office there with a sign on the door that read: "Have Adele Astair write a letter home for you." You could always find her, wearing the official Red Cross uniform, sitting in her office in the basement, writing letters for G.I.'S to their families in the states.

The Rainbow Center was the club where celebrities from the United States, members of the Royal family, and entertainers from England gathered to entertain soldiers on leave.

Lisa and Harry agreed they would share writing stories about the activities at the Rainbow Center. When Lisa had made her choices of the other clubs, Harry offered to accompany her around to introduce her to the people who would be of help in each of the clubs she had chosen. "But first," he suggested, "I think we should stop at the pub around the corner."

"You mean right now?" Lisa asked. "It's morning!"

"So?"

"But no one drinks in the morning."

"Ah...my dear," he explained. "You don't know the Continentals."

"Perhaps not," Lisa admitted, "but I think we should go to the clubs first, since this is my first day on the job."

"As you say," Harry acquiesced. "We can stop at the pub on the way back."

Lisa and Harry went first to the Milestone club where Lisa watched Harry at work bagging his daily quota of stories. His method was simple. He would sneak up on some unsuspecting GI who was lounging in one of the overstuffed chairs in the club. Invariably, the GI was wary, and you knew that he was thinking that Harry was a panhandler. But Harry, with great dignity, would announce himself as a reporter for the American Red Cross, and the interview would commence.

The whole interview took only a few minutes. Harry would ask a few questions about military status, name, address, home-town newspaper, length of service, past military campaigns, marital status, and the interview was over. But the story had barely begun. Harry composed the rest from the limitless reaches of his own imagination. Every American GI became a super-hero, engaged in extraordinary exploits, practically vanquishing the enemy single-handed. The soldier's home-town newspaper printed the story. The GI and his family were always proud and pleased, and Harry managed always to get in a plug for the American Red Cross club in London where our hero was having a happy time on R and R.

It wasn't a bad system, but Lisa couldn't do it. Her imagination was not as vivid as Harry's, and she was squeamish about fabricating stories, even for such a good cause.

Nevertheless, Lisa was enjoying her job. She found herself rushing from one activity to another, writing stories, and cooperating with the woman photographer who was employed by the Red Cross publicity department. It was a wonderful feeling to be doing a job that was fun and exciting and was filling a need for the soldiers in the American armed services.

However, Lisa was having difficulty finding a place to stay. She was still living at the Mount Royal Hotel, which was expensive, and not suited to her purposes. She wanted a small apartment where she could cook meals and live like a new bride, when and if Andy could come to London. During the war, housing in London was appallingly scarce. Many thousands of dwellings had been destroyed by bombs, and many hundreds of thousands of military personnel had surged into London from all over the world. It was almost impossible to find a roof over your head for a night, let alone for as long as Lisa needed one.

The situation might have continued for some time except for an unexpected health problem. One morning Lisa awoke with a severe stomach upset. She reported to the Red Cross doctor, Dr. McDonald, who told her that she was suffering from a severe case of morning sickness due to pregnancy.

"You won't send me home, will you?' she asked immediately.

Dr. McDonald, who was kind and understanding, looked thoughtful. "Do you have a husband?"

"Oh, yes," Lisa replied. "Indeed I do."

"I see no reason why you should be sent home then," he said with a relieved smile. "The war is almost over, the bombings have ceased, and I think you would do better over here with your husband than you would at home."

After the session with Dr. McDonald Lisa felt tired, and phoned Mr. McHenry at the office for permission to take the rest of the day off. After receiving permission, she returned to the Mount Royal Hotel and there standing in the lobby was a handsome young man wearing an air force leather flying jacket with silver wings on his chest, and captain's bars on his shoulders. He was smiling and holding out his arms, and Lisa was overwhelmed with joy. She needed Andy that evening, and a Guiding Hand had sent him to her.

When Lisa and Andy entered the bedroom, Lisa sat down on the bed, and Andy sat beside her. "You look tired," Andy said. "Are they working you too hard?"

"No," Lisa replied. "It isn't that. I'm pregnant."

"You're pregnant," Andy said. "That's wonderful!"

"It's wonderful that you're here,"Lisa said. "That's what's wonderful. I need you so much."

Andy took her in his arms. "I wouldn't leave you for a minute, if that were possible." he said.

The next morning Andy accompanied Lisa to the Publicity Office where they informed Mr. McHenry of Dr. McDonald's diagnosis. Mr. McHenry was encouraging. "Lisa can work here as long as she is able," he said. "And don't worry about an apartment. "We'll spread the word, and I'm sure someone will find a place for you. And Lisa, you can have the day off. You and Captain Thompson just go out and have a good time."

CHAPTER 25

DOLPHIN SQUARE

When Andy's two-day leave was over, Lisa knew that he would soon be flying missions again. "I've made arrangements with Lt. Winston to inform you whenever anything happens that I can't call," he said. "Lt. Winston is a good man, and he offered to do it for me."

"Yes, he's been a big help. But I'm praying he won't have to call me. For some reason his voice wouldn't give me the same lift that yours does."

Andy smiled, but soon turned serious again. "I wish I could help you find an apartment, and help you find a doctor, and do all of the other things an expectant father is supposed to do. It hurts me that I can't, because this is the fulfillment of all my hopes. I've got a wonderful wife and you'll have a wonderful baby, and I want so much to be at your side through it all. You know that?"

"Of course I do," Lisa said, "but you're doing more for me than the men over here whose wives are having babies in the States. Those poor guys won't see their babies until they get back home, and those girls will have their babies alone."

"Just the same," Andy said as he put his arms around Lisa, "I hate to think that I will leave tomorrow morning, and you must carry on alone."

When Lisa reported back to work after Andy had returned to his base, she discovered that there are many people around who are always ready to help when someone is in need. People who ordinarily might pass you by, suddenly become angels, offering help when it's most needed, and accepting nothing but your thanks and perhaps the warmth of knowing that they've helped to prove that there are far more good people in the world than bad ones.

Some English civilians, strangers to Lisa, had learned of her need for suitable housing, and had started scrounging about for a flat for her. Within a week, she was the grateful occupant of a three-room apartment in Dolphin Square.

Situated on the banks of the River Thames between London Bridge and Chelsea, Dolphin Square was a large apartment complex consisting of fourteen concrete and steel apartment houses, built around a city block. Inside the square were formal gardens and well-kept lawns that were always liberally decorated with ornate perambulators {prams} where the cradle set took its daily airing.

There were many nice amenities about Dolphin Square. There was, for instance, a swimming pool, a restaurant, and the ground floor of the main building which contained stores of all kinds. The apartments were comfortable and modern. All had central heating, fireplaces, and wall-speakers through which B.B.C. was piped from a master radio located elsewhere in the Square.

But best of all...the people who lived in Dolphin Square were friendly, and anxious to be kind. Strangers often stopped Lisa on the walk in the garden to ask if they could help her in any way. A registered nurse telephoned to offer her services if Lisa should need a nurse. A young office girl, Winnie Martin, telephoned Lisa the first time there was an air raid, and offered to sit with her. Lisa gratefully accepted her offer.

When there was nobody around in the evening, Lisa turned on the radio and listened to the highbrow music that was played incessantly between newscasts. Lisa wished that they would sometimes vary the program with a crooner or a cowboy singer or a jazz band.

Other than Prime Minister Churchill's "more sweat and tears" announcements and the King's words of encouragement, there were time announcements that were intriguing to Lisa. "It is now nine o'clock," the announcer would say, and then he would add: "or very nearly."

Dr. McDonald was wrong when he said the bombings were over. Very soon after Lisa was established in her apartment in Dolphin Square, the "Little Blitz" began. At first there were only a few planes flying over the city once in a while at night dropping bombs, but soon there were more, and before long they were coming in groups nearly every night. Whenever she was able to do so, Winnie came to sit with Lisa shortly after the air raid siren sounded off. But sometimes Winnie was on fire duty. On those nights, at the first sound of the siren, Winnie put on a tin helmet, armed herself with fire-fighting equipment and hurried to the roof top where she dashed about putting out fire bombs that the Germans dropped.

On those nights when Lisa was alone, she would think of Andy and wish that he was there to hold her in his arms. And despite all of her promises to be brave, she would find herself wondering if he had been on a mission, and she turned cold with fear when she thought that maybe he might not make it back.

When that happened, she found the loneliness unbearable so she turned out the lights and pulled the black-out curtains to watch what was going on in the dark skies over London.

Like a mammoth Fourth of July fireworks, the guns banged and crashed, ack-ack streaked across the sky and broke into shiny starlets, and sometimes the search lights "coned" a German plane. Lisa could see it diving and weaving in a desperate effort to get back into the safety of darkness as bursting shells sparked about it.

Other residents of Dolphin Square also watched out the windows, and they kept up a running comment on the progress of the shooting.

"Come now!"

"That's better!"

"No...a little more to the right."

"Dash it! Missed again."

Like rooting for the home team, Lisa thought, as she watched the plane get out of the cone and become lost in darkness.

A disappointed moan went up from the onlookers, but Lisa could not help being glad that the plane got away, and one more young flier had saved himself from an early death.

When the bombings got worse, and planes began coming in groups, and a battery of anti-aircraft guns across the river in Battersea Park opened up on them with a barrage of ack-ack, Lisa no longer watched out the window.

Instead, she sat in the big chair by the fireplace, listening to the sounds of war, trying to understand what was happening. During those nights she learned to admire the courage of English women. Just outside her second floor window there was an ambulance station, employing some ten or fifteen ambulances, all operated by young English girls. At the sound of the siren, the girls put on their tin helmets, ran to their ambulances, and Lisa could hear the engines start in readiness for the signal that sent ambulances to the scene of a bombing. There the girls worked with the air raid wardens rescuing victims and administering first aid, while ack-ack fell all about them. Lisa admired their bravery. Lisa also admired Winston Churchill's youngest daughter, Diane, and the other English women who were manning the anti-aircraft guns across the Thames in Battersea Park.

Despite the air raids, Lisa was settling into a new life very well. She was pleased with her flat; she liked her job in the Red Cross Publicity Office, and she was looking forward to the birth of a baby.

It was with a light heart that Lisa took advice from Winnie and other English friends to register with the government comprehensive health plan which furnished universal coverage for anyone who needed health services."And the best part, Winnie said, "It won't cost you anything."

All unsuspecting, Lisa braved the intricacies of the National Health Plan. She called Westminster Hospital for an appointment with an obstetrician. The telephone operator made an appointment for her, and dutifully, at the exact time specified, Lisa was sitting on a long hard bench in the cold and dismal hallway of Westminster Hospital. There were perhaps a hundred people there, and they all looked dreadfully ill. Lisa wasn't doing too well herself, afflicted as she was with morning sickness, noon-time sickness, and evening sickness. Nevertheless, she waited and waited. After several hours she was sure she had been exposed to every disease then current in London. She imagined that she was seeing infectious germs flying all about in the obnoxious smelling air. Trying to keep from vomiting herself, she had watched dozens of people vomiting, coughing and spitting, fainting and moaning, and bleeding. Finally she could stand it no longer and she got up and left.

When Lisa returned to her flat in early evening, she phoned Winnie to explain what had happened. "I'm not going back to that place," Lisa said. "If I have to, I'll have the baby right here in the flat, and we'll both die. But I'm not going back to that hell-hole."

Winnie was not as sympathetic as Lisa thought she would be. "You Americans have to realize that we don't have the luxuries that you've been used to," she said.

"Maybe so," Lisa replied, "But I'm not going back to that place. Maybe you can find a mid-wife for me. I've heard there are such people over here."

"Yes, I could do that," Winnie replied. "But there's another route. Some of the doctors have private offices which they've set up to take care of private patients during the hours they are not required to be on duty at the government Health Center. The only thing, they charge a lot of money."

"Somehow money doesn't seem so important when it's a matter of life or death," Lisa answered.

"English girls seem to do all right with the Comprehensive Health Service," Winnie said with a touch of irritation in her voice.

"Yes, but I'm not an English girl, and maybe I'm more susceptible to germs in the air," Lisa replied.

Winnie's irritation was perhaps understandable. By this time, Americans in England were no longer a novelty, and had become something of an annoyance. The English men, particularly, were fed up with American soldiers buying up all the spirits, renting the best flats, and monopolizing the English women. Some of the English men wise-cracked: "There are four things wrong with Americans... they're over-paid, over-dressed, over-sexed, and over here."

Lisa, however, was far too indebted to the kindness of the English people to feel any resentment about anything they said or did, even when she was humiliated when she offered a farthing to a bus conductoress as payment for her fare.

A farthing is a copper piece about the size of an American penny with a little bird engraved upon it. Shopkeepers gave them to customers as change, and that's how Lisa happened to have some in her purse. But she learned not to give them to a bus conductoress. "Farthings!" the bus conductoress exclaimed, loud enough to be heard throughout the bus. "I say, isn't that just like the blighted Yanks. Living off the fat `o the land, they are, and she gives me farthings!"

Embarrassed, because everyone in the bus seemed to be eyeing her with cold disapproval, Lisa slunk into the nearest seat. When Winnie came to see her that evening, Lisa asked Winnie what there was about farthings that you couldn't spend them.

"Most English people save them for charity," Winnie explained, "and the conductoress doesn't have a slot for them in her coin holder. However, since they're legal tender, she had to accept them."

Nevertheless, while the English were becoming increasingly annoyed with Americans, Lisa was settling more and more into English ways. She began to like tea better than coffee, and she was very fond of the mild-tasting fish and crispy chips which could be purchased without food stamps at fish counters around the city. Because of the shortage of paper during the war, the fish and chips were wrapped in newspapers. It was the dish that Lisa served to Andy when he showed up on her doorstep the first week-end after she moved into the flat. It was a wonderful evening.

Andy had not yet started missions and he was relaxed and happy. Even when the air raid siren sounded, Lisa and Andy were cuddled together on the sofa in front of the fireplace, drinking coffee, and enjoying the unexpected luxury of being together in the first home they had known. The sounds of anti-aircraft guns and falling bombs could not dim the joy that was in their hearts that night.

CHAPTER 26

AT HOME IN LONDON

Surprisingly, Andy managed to get to London much more than Lisa had ever thought possible."I work every angle I can think of to get here," he said, "and so far I've been doing pretty good."

Sometimes Andy brought guests with him, usually one of his pilot friends. Lisa would be hard pressed to find enough food to feed them. Somehow American men just didn't understand what it was like to be on English rations. Lisa's weekly food ration consisted of two mutton chops, a tablespoon of butter, two of lard, two of margarine, a quarter pound of cheese, two slices of bacon, and a half cup of sugar. Besides these items, she could buy ration-free sausage which was mostly cereal, fresh fish when available, powdered eggs, carrots, cabbage, and brussel sprouts. Also, because she was on an expectant-mother ration, she received a half pint of milk each day, and a fresh egg every three months.

On one occasion Andy called and informed Lisa that he had invited an American Major and the Major's friend, a Polish Countess, for Saturday evening dinner. Lisa had never entertained a countess before, and she was anxious to do Andy proud. She couldn't offer a half mutton chop, butterless potatoes, and brussel sprouts to a Countess.

In desperation, she got up early Saturday morning and rode a bus all the way across London to Maiden Lane Market where Winnie said she might be able to buy a bit of fish if she was lucky.

By the time Lisa arrived at the market, she was already tired from the long ride, and the rag-tag crowds of people, combined with the odors and hub-bub of merchants selling their wares, had started her overly-touchy stomach turning somersaults. She joined the first queue she saw, and was encouraged when she heard someone say it was a fish queue. Finally she came near the end of the line, and saw the vendor preparing a purchase for his customer. From a large box, he pulled out a thick, squirming eel, and with a long-bladed knife, deftly slashed the luckless thing straight down the middle. That did it. Lisa contributed the meager contents of her own stomach to the rest of the debris and odor of Maiden Lane Market, and caught a bus back to town.

Empty handed, feeling green, but with a stoicism above and beyond the call of duty, she stopped at Selfridges for a last try.

She was lucky. Selfridges was featuring a guinea hen that day, priced at 3.10.0.($14.00} which Lisa bought without blinking. At the green-grocer's she discovered a half dozen ears of golden bantam corn. When she caught the bus back to Dolphin Square, she felt fine, and was delighted with the success of her shopping excursion.

That wasn't all. One of the tenants in Dolphin Square who Lisa knew only slightly, knocked on Lisa's door and handed Lisa a bottle of rare dinner wine which she had saved throughout the war. "I know this is your first dinner party," the neighbor said, "and I hope this will help make it a success."

When Lisa and Andy Thompson's guests arrived that evening, Lisa immediately relaxed. The Countess was a petite woman, with dark hair and dark eyes, pretty in an unspectacular way, and so unassuming that Lisa felt at ease with her at once. And Andy pleased Lisa by being a most gracious host. Andy was happy and showed it. The tension lines were gone from his face, and he was laughing and joyful and showed his love for Lisa with open affection and praise for the dinner she had prepared.

Altogether the evening was a great success. Rare dinner wine, roasted stuffed guinea hen, corn-on -the-cob, and candlelight. What Countess could have asked for more?

As the Major and the Countess were leaving, the Countess unwittingly paid Lisa the greatest compliment. "I should like to repay your delicious dinner," the Countess said, "but I'm on English rations, you know."

Lisa was enjoying her new life at Dolphin Square. Andy was able to come home at least once a week. And to make life even more pleasant, Elsa, who Lisa had been missing more than she would have imagined, was soon transferred to London to assume an executive position with the aero club department. Although both girls were busy with their new jobs, Elsa and her friend Lt. Sampson, often called and joined Lisa and Andy for dinner.

And there was one very special evening when Lt. Winston called and invited Lisa and Andy to attend a ball for service men at the famous Covent Gardens where the Skyliner's Band was playing. It was a special occasion for

Lt. Winston and the members of his band which was gaining popularity throughout England, and had earned Lt. Winston a commendation from the Commanding General. Lisa and Andy by that time had both become jitterbug enthusiasts, as had most of the GIs and their English dates, and the Skyliner's band specialized in the wonderful jitterbug tunes: " In the Mood," "Blue Skies," "Long John Silver." Elsa was there dancing with Lt. Sampson. For Lisa it was a very special and happy reunion with friends who had shared an unforgettable adventure and a time in their lives that none of them would ever forget.

When all guests had returned to their bases, Lisa depended more and more on the companionship of Winnie, who shared her tea and cocoa rations with Lisa for evening snacks, and who calmed Lisa's fears during many harrowing hours when the air raids were in progress.

Lisa often had the feeling that Winnie had always known all of the things about having a baby that Lisa was trying to learn. Without ever having been married, Winnie knew all about being a wife. Without bearing children, Winnie knew how to prepare for the birth and care of a baby. She had learned it all from the infinite wisdom which was passed down by generations of hardy, self-sufficient mothers of the British North Country.

Lisa was sure that the Good Lord had sent Winnie to her in her time of need.

Lisa worked at the Red Cross Publicity Department much longer than she had thought would be possible. During the last few months before the birth of Lisa's baby, Harry cheerfully filled many of Lisa's interview obligations while Lisa stayed in the office and wrote copy. When Lisa finally quit, there were only a few days of her pregnancy left.

Although Lisa was sometimes very lonely and missed Andy dreadfully, there was one mitigating factor about living in an apartment in London away from the base. She was saved the agony of waiting for the sound of planes returning from a mission and the fear of hearing that Andy had not made it back.

CHAPTER 27

BABY BILL

The British obstetrician Lisa had engaged was Dr. Simms, one of four obstetricians on the staff of Westminster Hospital. Although Dr. Simms was perhaps one of the busiest men in all of London, he never seemed to be in a hurry, and always had time for some cheering words whenever Lisa visited his office on Harley Street. Lisa thought that the six hundred dollars she would pay to have a baby in England was a huge bargain.

On the first visit that Lisa made to Dr. Simms' office, she settled into a comfortable overstuffed chair to wait a few minutes for her appointment with the doctor. The waiting room was a pleasant well-furnished room with a magazine rack and newspaper stand. The nurse in attendance smiled and assured Lisa that the doctor would be with her in a few minutes. Lisa was glad that she was a spoiled American brat. "Everybody in the world should be so lucky as to be spoiled American brats," she thought.

Dr. Simms was unable to reserve a room for her in a hospital. "Women here book their hospital room as soon as they start thinking about having a baby," he explained. "If you aren't booked at least nine months ahead, you're out of luck."

As a result, Dr. Simms made arrangements for Lisa to have her baby in a nursing home in Hempstead.

It was a bad night, the night Lisa called for an ambulance to take her to the nursing home. She had made all necessary arrangements with the ambulance service, and had been assured that an ambulance would be ready when she needed one.

The air raids started early that night, and Winnie, who was sitting with Lisa, put down her knitting at the first undulating wail of the siren. "It's my night for fire-fighting," she said. "Why don't you go to bed now, and I'll look in when it's over."

"All right," Lisa said wearily. "I'm so tired of the raids, and tired of being pregnant, and tired of being frightened. I'm just tired, I guess."

"So are we all," Winnie replied as she left.

It was a bad raid. Lisa could hear the ack-ack falling like hail in the courtyard. The guns across the river were deafening, and now and then Lisa heard the sickening crash of a bomb hitting a target. And for the first time, she heard a bomb coming down, screaming past the window. She tried to get out of bed to stand in the doorway, because she knew that the bomb was close, and the door jam was supposed to protect one from falling debris. But she was slow and clumsy, and when the bomb landed in the next block, the concussion shook the building, and she fell.

Lisa was unhurt, but she was frightened, and she went back to bed, and waited for Winnie to come. She waited a long time, because it was a long raid. The planes came in waves, and the guns and the bombings banged on an on, and when the "All Clear" came, Lisa had already felt the first faint pains of childbirth.

When Winnie came at last, she looked so tired and wan, Lisa hesitated to tell her that labor pains had begun. Lisa knew that Winnie would have to go to work in the morning, and as it was, she would have only a few hours of sleep. But Winnie had to know. "I think I should call for an ambulance," Lisa said softly.

"The pains have started?" Winnie asked calmly.

"I think so."

"Well, you'd best call right away. I doubt that you'll get one though. It was a bad raid tonight, and every ambulance must be out."

"But I made arrangements," Lisa protested in alarm. "I was told they would send one when I called."

"Just the same, you'd best call."

Winnie was right. When Lisa called the ambulance service, a girl informed her that all of the ambulances were out. "We'll send one as soon as possible," she promised.

When the phone rang at 3:00 A.M., Lisa thought it would be the ambulance service informing her that they were sending the ambulance out. However, it was Elsa on the phone. Elsa, too, was in trouble. She had been bombed out of her rooming house, and she wanted to know if she could stay with Lisa until she could find another room.

"Of course you can," Lisa said, "but I'm leaving for the hospital shortly."

"You're having the baby tonight?" Elsa asked.

"If I ever get an ambulance," Lisa replied.

"I'll be right out," Elsa said. "And Lisa, would you mind if I borrow one of your uniforms? Everything I own was lost. I could only save my dance dress and shoes, and my overcoat and pajamas."

"You're welcome to anything I own," Lisa replied. "But where are you now and what are you wearing?" Lisa had visions of Elsa out in the cold without proper clothes.

"I'm at the Embassy Club in my dance dress, " Elsa answered, laughing. "And I've been dancing with a most elegant Colonel."

"I might have known," Lisa said.

When Lisa put down the phone, there was a knock at the door. It was the night boy, reporting that an ambulance was outside.

"Let Elsa into the flat when she comes," Lisa instructed Winnie, "and tell her to get in touch with Andy."

As the ambulance wound its way from Dolphin Square along the bank of the River Thames, Lisa noted with horror that the opposite bank was a mass of flames for as far as she could see.

"They always bomb that side of the river," the driver explained, because they want to knock out the industrial plants over there."

"It looks like they did quite a job tonight," Lisa replied.

At the Hempstead Nursing Home the driver carried Lisa's suitcase into the building, and gave it to a youthful nurse who led Lisa to an upstairs room. It was a large room, and very cold because it was heated by a sixpence eating heater, and Lisa was expected to furnish the sixpences. It was, however, a comfortable, homey room, with a large window overlooking a garden. Lisa didn't notice these things immediately, however, because her fascinated gaze was directed towards an empty baby crib in the room.

As if she were reading Lisa's mind, the nurse remarked: "A baby will be there when I come back on duty this evening."

The nurse was right. A baby boy was there when she came back on duty, and a lot had gone on in the interim.

Captain Thompson had arrived from the base, and was in the room with Lisa, holding her hand through the labor pains until the doctor told him to leave. Andy and the doctor were in disagreement. Andy thought that Lisa should be given pain-killers "like they do in the States."

Dr. Simms was determined that he should deliver the baby without pain-killers, "like they do in England."

The doctor won, and Captain Thompson was banished from the room to the downstairs sitting room.

Lisa saw her son a few seconds after he was born, when the matron held him up to the window to inspect him. "He has lovely brown hair," she said.

He had a mass of brown hair all right, on a head that had been smashed to a point. Lisa's first sight of him made her forget all the agony of the hours before. "I've been punished for every sin I ever committed," she moaned. "He's got something wrong with him, hasn't he?"

"No," the matron replied, "He's a fine, handsome lad."

But Lisa wasn't so sure, and she suddenly felt very tired, and fell into a troubled sleep. When she awoke, the doctor was still there, working with the baby, and she heard him say; "Did anyone tell that poor bloke downstairs that he has a son?"

"For Heavens sake, somebody tell him," Lisa said.

When Andy came into the room, smiling and happy, Lisa thought it all had been worth whatever it took. Andy had a son and heir, and that was his fondest wish. Lisa thanked God for keeping Andy safe so he could see his son.

Andy and Lisa named their son William, because he was born in England, and William seemed like a good name for a young man who was part English and mostly American.

"We'll call him Bill" Andy said.

Bill's looks improved hourly. Lisa could almost see him changing as he lay in his crib beside her bed. His head rounded out, his skin paled, and he looked more and more like the son of a handsome man like Andy should look.

The Hempstead Nursing Home was an old mansion that had not undergone any physical changes from the time it was a family home. The only concession it made to its new function, was the addition of a surgical table which was pushed into the room when the baby was born. This equipment was immediately removed, and the home-like atmosphere continued.

Nurses treated their charges like members of a big family, and amused themselves and their patients by carrying babies from one room to another to show them off, cooing over them and announcing each as a "lovely baby."

Lisa liked having Bill in the room with her all during the day. She could watch him as he slept, and could pick him up and cuddle him when he awoke. After the ten o'clock feeding at night, however, all of the babies were taken to a room downstairs; and sometimes, if there was an early air raid, the nurses took the babies sooner, so they would be on the first floor for easier evacuation.

It was always traumatic for Lisa when they took Bill away during an air raid. She felt she should be near him so she could protect him from danger.

The nurses at the Hempstead Home worked shockingly hard, and for long hours at a time. There were only two day nurses and one night nurse to care for twelve mothers and thirteen babies. The matron helped when she could, but she was busy herself keeping records and helping the doctor during births.

The nurses were required to make the beds, bathe and medicate the patients, carry food trays up and down the four flights of stairs, feed the babies and wash their diapers in the bathtub and hang them over a screen in front of the fireplace to dry. Lisa marvelled that they complained so little, and she thought they deserved a medal for serving tea twice a day between meals. But this, she supposed, was in accordance with English custom, which never changes.

Elsa came to see Lisa soon after Bill was born, and for once Elsa's candor was not equal to the situation. She wanted very much to say something nice about Lisa's baby, and wound up by observing weakly: "All babies are cute."

However, Lisa was by then so much encouraged by the improvement in Bill's appearance, that she didn't mind Elsa's lack of enthusiasm. Elsa just doesn't know anything about new babies, she thought, and couldn't be expected to know that Bill was really quite special.

Winnie came to see Lisa too, and brought Bill his first toy, a fuzzy teddy bear. There were other gifts and letters from people in the Red Cross, and one day someone sent a box of groceries. In it was a dozen eggs, butter, coffee, fruit juice, and a bottle of wine. It was, of course, quartermaster supplies, sent by someone who was concerned that Lisa would not have enough to eat when she returned to her flat in Dolphin Square.

When it was time to take Bill home, Lisa was greatly relieved because the apartment at Dolphin Square was much safer then the old mansion he was born in, and by then there were nightly air raids over London.

As soon as Lisa entered the door of her flat with Bill he began to be like a hot potato. He was forever crying because he was hungry. This was a dilemma for Lisa. The nurses had warned her against feeding him between feeding times. "Just make him wait until the next feeding," they said.

Finally Lisa sought the advice of the American Red Cross doctor, Dr. McDonald. "The English believe in discipline, even for babies," he said. "but in America we feed a hungry baby."

Lisa followed Dr. McDonald's advice and her troubles with Bill ended. Bill had been born in England, but he acted like an American, and this was a source of some satisfaction to Lisa.

Bill, because he was born in England, had "dual" citizenship. At age twenty one, he could choose if he would be British or American. There was never any doubt in Lisa's mind that he would choose to be an American, as any person in his right mind would. But Winnie was not so sure. "It is the greatest thing in the world to be born a British citizen," Winnie said with conviction.

CHAPTER 28

BRAINTREE, BUZZ-BOMBS AND V-2

Lisa's three month's leave of absence from the American Red Cross was over too soon. Lisa dreaded leaving Dolphin Square. It had become home to her, and she was ever so grateful to the staff and friendly tenants who had made her happy during her stay there. Nevertheless, she dutifully reported to headquarters and was told to "await further orders."

Lisa was re-assigned to be the director of the enlisted men's club in the town of Braintree, near the base where Andy was stationed. Once again, compassionate and caring officials at the American Red Cross headquarters had made it possible for Lisa and Andy to spend as much time as possible together.

Andy, during his off-duty hours, had rented a spare room in a private home, where the Hannett family lived, several blocks from the club where Lisa was to be stationed. It was an ideal arrangement because the Hannett family agreed to care for baby Bill while Lisa was working. Mr. and Mrs. Hannett and their two daughters, Mary, sixteen, and Jill, twelve, soon became family to Lisa and Andy, and to their son, Bill. Together, they faced the next months of the war. They worried with Lisa when Andy was not able to call as soon as they expected after he had returned from a mission, and comforted her until his safe return. And they all loved little Bill, and cared for him as if he were one of their own.

The American Red Cross enlisted men's club which Lisa directed, had been established a year before in a large building on a tree-lined street. It was called "The Institute," and before the war, had been a town library and gathering place for the townspeople. There was a large hall, with tables and chairs, and a long serving counter where the Red Cross staff served coffee, doughnuts, sandwiches and snacks and Coca-Cola which was bottled in town and sometimes contained drowned honey bees floating at the top of the bottle. All of the food was prepared in a large restaurant-type kitchen, which had been equipped with the inevitable Red Cross doughnut-making machine. At one end of the hall was a stage, where the band played when a dance was scheduled.

Behind the main building, across an alley, were large dormitories where American enlisted men could stay who were on leave or on an overnight pass. The dormitories were under the supervision of a local man who hired and directed the help.

Lisa was surprised on her first day at the club to find several German P.O.W.'s and their American guard who could speak German, eating lunch in the kitchen. The P.O.W.'s had been recruited to do the heavy cleaning in the dormitories and the club. Even more surprising to Lisa were the English girls on the staff who were giving their own cigarettes to the German soldiers. The German soldiers with tears in their eyes, were showing the girls pictures of their wives and children in Germany.

It was the first time that Lisa had thought of German soldiers as anything other than "the enemy." These men were so startingly young and sad, and so anxious to be friendly, that Lisa, too, was moved to feel sorry for them. For the first time Lisa realized that Germans were also victims of the war.

Lisa had assumed that her move to the country would relieve her of the nightly terror of air raids, and she was right. But what she had not counted on was a new Nazi weapon which became known as a buzz-bomb, that flew by itself without anyone in it. Nor could she have dreamed that Braintree was located in what was to become known as "Buzz-bomb Alley." The little village of Braintree was in a direct line between the Nazi Buzz-Bomb launching site on the Continent and London where the bombs were designed to run out of gas, fall down, and explode.

Andy was staying with Lisa in town when they heard the air raid warning one night after they had gone to bed. Little Bill was already asleep in his crib. Lisa and Andy arose and pulled the black-out curtains to watch. It was a buzz-bomb, and chills ran down Lisa's spine at the first unearthly grinding sound of the thing. "It's weird," she whispered.

As the sound grew louder, they peered intently into the darkness, and soon a fire-like glow appeared at the end of the lane, and they could make out the dark form of the buzz-bomb. It was a great black bomb, flying just above the tree tops, flames shooting out behind it, and the crude engine grinding with such intensity that the noise shook the earth.

Lisa was too frightened to say anything, but Andy laughed. "Those Krauts just won't give up," he said. "But they're too late. No matter what they do, it's about over for them. Our missions are cake walks now. They don't even have the guns or ammunition to shoot us down any more."

Andy pulled Lisa into his arms. "You know, sweetheart. I think I'm going to make it through this damned war," he said.

But Lisa and Andy and the other inhabitants of Braintree were not through with buzz-bombs yet, nor with another Nazi weapon known as V-2.

The Hannett family, and Bill and Lisa, were as well equipped for a bombing as was possible in a little cottage in the country. They all had gas masks, even Bill, who was equipped with a bag-like contraption with an isinglass window and an air pump. In case of a poison gas attack, which the British thought the Germans would very likely attempt as a last resort, Lisa was instructed to put on her own mask first, and then put Bill in the bag and keep pumping air in to him.

The former dining room downstairs in the Hannett home had been converted into a gas-proof shelter. All of the windows were sealed and covered. The door could be sealed in case of emergency, and the room was equipped with a Morrison Shelter. This was an iron table with steel sides, which was strong enough to hold the weight of a falling house. It was a simple device, designed by Herbert Morrison, and it saved thousands of people from being crushed to death during the bombings in England.

The two young Hannett girls, Mary and Jill, slept under the Morrison shelter at night, and when the buzz-bombs were flying close, Lisa sometimes took Bill down and put him in the shelter with them. One frightful night, a buzz-bomb flying directly over the Hannett house was under attack by two R.A.F. fighters who were trying to shoot it down and making a terrible commotion. Lisa snatched Bill from his crib and ran downstairs to safety under the Morrison shelter. Fortunately the bomb missed the house, but it was just one more terror of the kind that the families in England faced night and day. Brave R.A.F. pilots often tried to knock the buzz-bombs down by flying alongside and tipping the bomb with a nudge from the wings of their planes.

The V-2 bombs came after the buzz-bombs had run their course, and were, in many ways, more frightening than the buzz-bombs had been. The V-2 bombs were missiles which reached England from the Continent so fast that there was not time for a raid warning before they hit and exploded. Several landed near Braintree, but most were destined for London and caused great damage there.

But Andy was right. It was too little too late for the Germans. Plans were being laid all over England for a massive invasion of the Continent which would be the end of Hitler and the war. Everywhere you went, wherever you looked, there were men and women in uniform who were being organized into invasion forces.

CHAPTER 29

D-DAY

The date of the invasion of the Continent was one of the most gigantic of secrets. The entire population of England, and all of the hundreds of thousands of allied people who were there for military reasons, were to be like the three monkeys. They were to see no invasion preparations, hear no invasion preparations, and speak of no invasion preparations.

If there was a successful element of surprise in the invasion, it was because everyone kept faith. Although preparations were going on all about, and although everyone was deeply interested in the outcome, no one talked about it.

It was June 4, 1944, and Lisa knew that invasion time had arrived when she noted that all military personnel were leaving the club in the early evening, and she saw Andy coming in the door to walk with her down the country lane to the Hannett cottage. As they were walking along between the hedge rows that lined the alley, Andy put his arm around Lisa's waist. "I won't be staying tonight," he said. "The base has been restricted. But I wanted to see Bill before I left. I hope he's still awake.".

Lisa didn't reply. She knew that the invasion was imminent, and she could not talk for fear of breaking into tears. She knew she had to be brave for Andy's sake.

When Andy and Lisa arrived at the cottage, Mrs. Hannett told them that Bill was already in his crib, sound asleep. Lisa and Andy quietly walked up the stairway to their room, and approached the crib. Andy stood looking at his sleeping son for a long time. Finally, Andy turned to Lisa with a question: "Do you think he looks like me?"

"The spitting image," Lisa replied.

Andy smiled. "That's good to know," he said, as he took Lisa's hand and led her towards the bed. Lisa was crying. She couldn't help it. "Don't cry,

Lisa," Andy said. "This is the beginning of the end of the war. It's a time for hope and the promise of a future for us."

After Andy left for his base, Lisa lay awake until dawn, expecting anytime to hear the drone of planes, marking the beginning of the invasion of the Continent. But the time had not arrived, yet.

Along with the rest of the population in England at that time, Lisa waited all through that day, but it was not until the early morning of the following day, June 6, that she heard the drone of hundreds of planes in the sky. She ran outside to watch, and was awed at the sight of a sky filled with planes as far as the eye could see. "Take care, Andy," she said. "Don't run into anyone."

Then Lisa sat on the wooden swing in the garden and bent her head to pray. She prayed for Andy to return safely, and she prayed for the American soldiers who she knew at that moment were landing on the beaches of the Continent.

It was early afternoon on that same day, June 6. Lisa was at the club, sitting at her desk staring at the empty tables in the dining hall, when Andy called to tell her he was safely home. "I told you I was going to make it," he said. "I'll be there for dinner at the White Hart Hotel tonight. It's a good time for a celebration."

The celebration that evening at the White Hart Hotel dining room was great. Andy was up-beat about the invasion. "We're going to drive those Krauts back where they belong," he said, "and we're going home again to a wonderful life."

Andy had ordered the usual gin and bitters drink and he lifted his glass for the usual toast. "To our love forever."

After D-Day, everyone waited breathlessly for word that allied troops were securely entrenched. Then Lisa and other care-takers in England began to make preparations to care for the wounded and exhausted who came back. An American station hospital was located a mile out of Braintree, and soon the club in town was crowded with men who leaned on crutches, who were wrapped in bandages, and who stared from shell-shocked eyes.

The men from the hospital were replacing the men of the Air Force who were leaving for new bases on the Continent.

Then one day Andy came into the club looking sad, and Lisa knew he had orders to leave, too. When he walked into her office Lisa said, "You don't have to tell me. I know."

"I came to tell you good-bye," he said. "There's a command car outside waiting to take me back to the base. I only have time for a kiss, and a pledge that I'll be loving you and little Bill forever."

During the following months, Lisa worked hard to accommodate the patients from the military hospital and the men from the only B-17 bomber group still in England near the club.

There seemed to be a general morale let-down in the military personnel and also in the English population, because a war that was supposed to be over, was dragging on. The news of the Battle of the Bulge was discouraging. It was demoralizing to know that there was still fighting ability in the Nazi forces and they were still attacking and killing allied men.

Andy had been wrong about it being a cake-walk. Reports were coming in from the wounded men who returned that there was fierce fighting at Bastogne, and the city was surrounded by Nazi tanks. The Allied forces had been taken unaware by the Nazi effort to divide the allied forces and to force surrender. The casualties in the airborne, air force and ground forces were far greater than expected. Christmas came and went with little notice. The news of the fighting on the Continent was so bad that no one felt like celebrating while American and British men were dying on foreign soil.

Andy was writing whenever he could, but his letters were often delayed, which caused almost unbearable anxiety for Lisa. She was concerned when his letters were brief and without reports of any kind. If any of the news was good, she was sure Andy would tell her because he wouldn't want her to worry. But Lisa did worry when she heard reports of the fighting at Bastogne in Belgium, because she knew Andy was stationed "somewhere" in Belgium, and she knew he would be engaged in the fighting. Also, Lisa missed her friends and co-workers in the American Red Cross who were joining the Allied forces on the Continent.

Elsa, too, came to Braintree to tell Lisa she was leaving soon. And one day Lisa's former field director, Mickey Stutz, dropped in to tell her good-bye, and to surprise her by saying: "I wish you were going over with us, Lisa. You were the best club director I ever had."

Lisa answered quite truthfully: "Thanks, Mickey. You were the best field director I ever had. Good Luck."

Because of falling morale, there were many quarrels in the club most of which Lisa could break up. But one evening while a dance was in progress, an organized group of paratroopers from the military hospital started a fight with the Air Force men at the dance. Before Lisa could get the M.P.'s there to break it up, several men were knocked out, five dance hostesses had fainted, and blood was splattered all about the floor.

When the M.P.'s arrived, Lisa stood with the Sergeant in the center of the hall, and pointed out the men she wanted him to arrest. "Arrest that one, and that one, and that one," she ordered as she shook with anger.

Next day, however Lisa was able to forgive the paratroopers to the extent that she did not press charges against them. She remembered several months before when she had seen these same paratroopers on their way to the Continent. Hundreds of gliders had flown over Braintree that day, flying so slow and so low that she could see the men huddled against the windows. She thought then that it must take a great deal of courage to drop out of a glider inside enemy lines. Lisa felt that she owed them a debt, and she tried to repay it.

It was a terrible winter...cold...cold. Snow fell in November, and did not thaw again until spring. Trudging home at midnight after she had closed the club, became a nightly ordeal for Lisa. It was always spooky walking along the hedge-row lined Lane. The snow froze, and she could hear her own footsteps as she walked along. Sometimes it was so cold it seemed to Lisa that the air itself was frozen, because it was thick, and her breath came back in her face and froze there. And it was so dark that even the white of the snow failed to penetrate the blackness.

Usually Lisa held the light of her torch just ahead of her feet, but sometimes she would cover the light with her hand, and would walk a way in the dark, trying to convince herself that she was therefore invisible to whatever terror was lurking behind the hedges. But it was no good. The crunch of her overshoes breaking through the frozen snow echoed along the narrow Lane, and gave her away.

Then Lisa would take her hand from in front of the torch, and would flash it ahead, searching for the lonely little church on the left, which was the half-way mark between the beginning of the Lane, and the Hannett home. When she reached the church she tried not to look in the window at the strange blue light that glowed there like a candle in front of a sepulchre. But she always looked, just to see if it was still there, and it always was.

After that, on her right, she soon passed the vicarage where the vicar lived alone, secluded by hedges and evergreens, locked behind tight shuttered windows so that no light shone through. But Lisa knew that somewhere inside, the vicar was in his office writing murder mysteries, which he published under a nom de plume, as if his secret were not known to everyone in the village. Past the vicarage, Lisa was soon at the Hannett house which was at the far end, where the Lane ended with a turnstile.

Then one night it happened. Lisa had almost reached the church, when she realized with a cold, sinking feeling in the pit of her stomach, that she was being followed. She could hear the footsteps behind her, breaking through the snow. She started to run as fast as she could go, and strangely, she held her own, and managed to reach the porch, and unlock the door. She was safely inside before the man could catch up with her. It was a close call, but by then Lisa had become used to close calls.

Lisa was surprised and pleased one day in early spring when she received a message from the American Red Cross Clubmobile girls who sent a card from "somewhere" across the Channel. It read: "Dear Lisa. We have just served coffee and doughnuts to Andy. He's O.K. but missing you, and sends his love."

The Doughnut Dollies were on the job, and Lisa was grateful. Their message, however, was the last Lisa would receive from Andy. A few days later, Lisa was sitting at her desk, looking out over the dining hall, when she saw Captain Winston and Elsa walking towards her office. Without asking, Lisa knew the reason for their visit. Once again, she felt pain-killing numbness surge over her mind and body.

When Captain Winston and Elsa reached her office door, Lisa spoke in a monotone without emotion: "You don't have to tell me. I know. Is there any hope?"

"The report was that no-one saw any parachutes." Captain Winston said gently.

Elsa put her arms around Lisa. "Remember what you told me when it was Larry," she said. "You said I had a job to do."

"Yes," Lisa answered quietly, "but not for me this time. I can't do any more. I will call the headquarters tomorrow morning and ask to be sent home."

"We understand," Captain Winston said, and Lisa was surprised to note that there were tears in his eyes.

Elsa, too, was crying. "Someday maybe we'll get out of this hell-hole," she said.

Lisa looked up and spoke slowly. "I've been thinking," she said."I've been thinking about Steve, and Larry, and now Andy, and all of the hundreds of thousands of other young men and women who are gone...all because of one strange little German man with a silly mustache and waving arms, ranting and raving. There has to be a way to stop his kind before they get out of hand."

"We'll work on that when we meet again in San Francisco," Captain Winston said.

Lisa was surprised. "Do you plan to be in San Francisco?" she asked.

"Yes, I've sent in an application for a job on your old newspaper, the Examiner."

"I didn't know you were a newspaperman, " Lisa said. "Why didn't you tell me?"

"You didn't ask, " Captain Winston replied with a wry smile.

"Maybe we'll be co-workers again," Lisa said. "I would like that. You were a very good Commanding Officer. I couldn't have done without you. Next time maybe I won't have to salute."

"I didn't notice you saluting this time," Captain Winston reminded her.

Elsa entered the conversation, "And that isn't all. I'm planning to be in San Francisco, too. Lt. Sampson and I have been talking, and we're hoping to open a dance studio there if everything works out."

Before Lisa could get over the surprise of it all, she looked up and saw Harold Cross walking across the dining hall towards her office. Lisa stood to greet him: "How glad I am to see you. You aren't a spy after all. Or are you? How did you know about Andy?"

"I heard this morning," Harold answered. I came to say I'm very sorry, and to tell you that we'll meet again in San Francisco. I will be going home shortly. My job here is about over."

"It will be so good to see you all again in San Francisco."Lisa said.

Captain Winston reached to take Lisa's hand. "Elsa and I have to leave," he said. "The Colonel arranged for us to fly over to see you, but we have to get right back. It's getting a little rough over there."

"Take care of yourselves," Lisa said. "I've missed you."

"We'll see you in San Francisco," Harold said, as he, too, turned to leave.

Several days later, Lisa received orders to be ready to leave Braintree. In the morning an American Red Cross car and a driver were waiting for her at the door of the club. Lisa was ready. She had carefully packed the footlocker and suit-case with as much of the memorabilia of her life in England as she could stuff in. What was left, the Hannetts said they would store for her at their home.

"We'll get together after the war is over," they promised.

Lisa and Bill were driven to a military hospital on the South coast of England. From there they were sent aboard a hospital ship with several hundred wounded soldiers and the doctors and nurses who cared for them. It was an uneventful trip. All passengers were restricted to their staterooms where meals were served to them. There were no shipboard activities to relieve the monotony.

When the ship approached New York harbor, Lisa carried Bill to the top deck where she was comforted when she saw the Statue of Liberty welcoming her back to the friendly shores. Then she cuddled Bill in her arms and carried him down the steps to the lower deck and back to the stateroom to "await further orders" for the last time.

THE AMERICAN RED CROSS

This story, "Doughnut Dollies," is meant to be a tribute to The American Red Cross...that wonderful American institution that answers the call for help whenever and wherever it is heard. Its members sail into uncharted waters, enter into unknown situations, doing their best to rescue people in distress. Because they are just ordinary people like you and me, sometimes they are tried beyond their capabilities, but they always respond when the call for help is heard.